Hunter broke off the kiss.

He leaned his head back to stare at her. "Don't do this, Bailey. The heat is only aftershocks of adrenaline running through you. It isn't real. You'd hate yourself later for giving in to it. Worse, you'd hate me."

"I could never hate you."

Caught between paradise and hell, Hunter hesitated. How could he have forgotten the pull of her kiss, the sensation of having her breasts pressed against him? The answer was simple. He hadn't forgotten at all, but had pushed the memories into a distant recess of his mind to save his sanity and maintain the harmony in his life.

He wasn't about to go through that again. Not even for the promise of what he held in his arms.

**Start off the New Year right—
with four heart-pounding romances from
Silhouette Intimate Moments!**

- Carla Cassidy's WILD WEST BODYGUARDS miniseries continues with *The Bodyguard's Return* (#1447).

- RaeAnne Thayne's *High-Risk Affair* (#1448) is a no-risk buy—we guarantee you'll love it!

- *Special Agent's Seduction* (#1449), the latest in Lyn Stone's SPECIAL OPS miniseries, is sure to please.

- Linda Conrad's NIGHT GUARDIANS keeps going strong with *Shadow Hunter* (#1450).

And starting next month, Silhouette Intimate Moments will have a new name,

Silhouette Romantic Suspense.

Four passionate romantic suspense novels each and every month.

Don't miss a single one!

Linda Conrad

SHADOW HUNTER

Silhouette®

INTIMATE MOMENTS™

Published by Silhouette Books

America's Publisher of Contemporary Romance

To John Fowler, who graciously allowed the rest of us to
sleep easier. We're so grateful to have you in the family.
We love you, John!

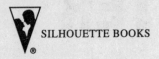 SILHOUETTE BOOKS

ISBN-13: 978-0-373-27520-5
ISBN-10:   0-373-27520-X

SHADOW HUNTER

Copyright © 2007 by Linda Lucas Sankpill

Visit Silhouette Books at www.eHarlequin.com

Printed in U.S.A.

Books by Linda Conrad

Silhouette Intimate Moments

*Shadow Force #1413
*Shadow Watch #1418
*Shadow Hunter #1450

Silhouette Desire

The Cowboy's Baby Surprise #1446
Desperado Dad #1458
Secrets, Lies...and Passion #1470
The Gentrys: Cinco #1508
The Gentrys: Abby #1516
The Gentrys: Cal #1524
Slow Dancing With a Texan #1577
The Laws of Passion #1609
Between Strangers #1619
†*Seduction by the Book* #1673
†*Reflected Pleasures* #1679
†*A Scandalous Melody* #1684

*The Gentrys
†The Gypsy Inheritance
**Night Guardians

LINDA CONRAD

was inspired by her mother, who gave her a deep love of story telling. "Mom told me I was the best liar she ever knew. And that's saying something for a woman with an Irish-storyteller's background," she says. Linda has been writing contemporary romances for Silhouette for six years. Besides telling stories, her passions are her husband and family, and finding the time to read cozy mysteries and emotional love stories. Linda keeps busy and is happy living in the sunshine near the Florida Keys. Visit Linda's Web site at http://www.lindaconrad.com/

Dear Reader,

The Navajo people have a rich tradition of legend and storytelling. I have taken the liberty of using some of their grand traditions as a base for making up my own legends. Much of what you read in this series is as it has been told to me. The rest is from my imagination. The People call their philosophy, "Walking in Beauty." Walk in beauty with Hunter and Bailey as they find lost loves...and the truth that lies within them.

Some readers may need a refresher on Dine words, so here is a short vocabulary list:

Dine	The Navajo—also known as The People
Dinetah	The land between the four "sacred" mountains where legend says the Dine began and where many of them now live (the "four corners" Big reservation that encompasses parts of Arizona, New Mexico, Colorado and Utah)
amá sání	grandmother (maternal)
anali	grandmother (paternal)
atsili	younger brother
azee'	medicine
bilagaana	white (as in "white man")
chindi	The dark spirits that come with death
hastiin	mister, the title for a respected clan elder
hataalii	medicine man
hogan	The traditional housing of the Navajo, built in an eight-sided round design and now mostly used for religious purposes
ya'at'eeh	hello
Yei	The gods of Navajo myths

Best wishes,

Linda

Prologue

Night, that insidious thief of light, plundered her reality and stole the resolve so hard won by daylight.

Bailey Howard leaned her forehead against the cool window of the air-conditioned bus and swallowed the bitter taste of panic. She would gladly kill for a glass of chardonnay right about now. Wine wouldn't have been her drug of choice, but the wish for booze was better than wishing for the line of coke she'd really been craving.

And had vowed to never have again.

She opened her eyes to the inky darkness reflecting back her own haggard image in the glass. What in hell was she doing on a damn bus, having spooky shivers in the middle of a heat wave?

Buses were certainly not her style. What would her New York buddies have to say about such a thing?

She'd been out of the loop for the last five months,

holed up at the Renaissance Malibu Rehab Center. So Bailey would be willing to bet none of those New York people would recognize her at all by now. Just as well. They were history. Her history.

But as the word *history* ran through her head, she remembered a more distant past. A time when she couldn't wait for the lazy, hot summer to bring her back to her grandmother's house in the Arizona mountains of the "big" Navajo reservation in the Four Corners area.

Well, it was a hot summer once again. But she dreaded going to Anali's rustic cabin in the trees this time. Dreaded having to see her grandmother when there was every possibility she would not even be able to recognize her only granddaughter's face.

God, how Bailey hated this. She didn't want to think of putting her grandmother into a nursing home and then packing up her belongings, along with all her memories. It wasn't fair. How could life be so cruel?

She took a slow breath and tried again to peer out through the black night, but only managed another irritated glimpse of her own reflection in the glass. As a topper to one of the worst times of her entire life, she might've known the damn airlines would manage to screw up. They'd landed the plane at the Flagstaff airport so late that none of the car rental places were still open.

The Labor Day holiday weekend meant none of the motels in the area had any vacancies, either. So here she was. With an intrepid band of passengers, heading down the dark highway through the midnight hours. Her airline shuttle bus was making its way toward Farmington, New Mexico, on the far edge of the Navajo reservation and the closest city to her grandmother's home.

Bailey planned to complain loudly about the screwup. Maybe she would even sue. The very minute she got off this damn bus.

Giving up on the black void outside the window, she stretched her legs and pushed the small of her back against the seat in an effort to ease her cricks and aches. If it were only a bit warmer. Or if only she had a blanket.

Thunk. "Ow." *Thunk. Thunk.*

"Damn it," she yelled, turning around to address the woman in the row behind her. "Can't you keep that kid from kicking the seat back? I'm trying to sleep."

The toddler's mother, a Mexican-American girl barely out of her teens, looked embarrassed. "Sorry. Tara needs a bottle to sleep and I didn't bring enough. I didn't think we'd be traveling so long."

Bailey got up, trying to stay warm. "Don't you have some emergency supplies? You can't expect to travel with a kid who's…" she waved her hand at the baby "…how old?"

"Tara's almost a year old. My husband's unit was called up, so we're going to stay with his parents until he comes back to the States."

Tiny Tara, who must've had the biggest chocolate-colored eyes in existence, heard her name and began screaming and wriggling in earnest.

"Sheesh, Tara. This is so not cool." The mother stood with the crying baby in her arms. "I've got a box of apple juice I can put in a bottle. Maybe that will work. It'll only take me a second to fix it up."

Before Bailey knew what was happening, the young woman shoved the kid toward her chest and released her. Bailey had no choice but to capture the squirming baby in her arms.

"Hey," she exclaimed as she hung on to the kicking kid. "What do you think you're doing?"

"Hold her a minute while I get the bottle ready." The young woman pulled out a large bag. "You might try walking Tara up and down the aisle. Maybe that will calm her."

"Me?"

The mother didn't answer. She didn't even glance up as she continued digging in her oversize and intensely ugly flowered satchel.

Trying to arrange the child on her shoulder, Bailey turned and headed for the rear of the bus. Terrific. What she knew about babies would fit into a tequila shot.

She looked around at the half-dozen other passengers for help. Nobody moved.

A minute of holding the brat couldn't be that bad, right? Bailey took a few steps, jiggling the baby in her arms. But the bus rounded a sharp curve just then, and she was thrown off balance.

"The ride's getting rough, kid. We've gotta hang on."

Plopping down into an empty seat a few rows behind her own, Bailey once again glanced toward the dark glass beside her. It seemed that the driver was suddenly having trouble staying on the road.

A pair of red-rimmed, yellow eyes appeared at her window. *Honestly.* Two eyes, no face.

Ohmigod. Was she hallucinating? Five months of rehab and *now* she was seeing things?

Gasping, Bailey looked around to see if anyone else had seen it, too. Everyone seemed to be asleep.

She must be exhausted. She must be overly stimulated. Oh, hell. She must be downright insane.

That did it. She had to get some sleep. Now.

She prepared to get back on her feet. Her knees were knocking together so badly, though, that she hesitated at the edge of her seat for a second before feeling strong enough to get herself and the baby up.

She waited one moment too long.

Chapter 1

Navajo Tribal Special Investigator Hunter Long had been called in the middle of a terrifying dream—of a Skinwalker with the face of his dead father. One of *those* dreams. He was actually glad to have been awakened from it.

Dazed, he'd dressed and driven to the subagency office at Chinle as dawn began peeking around the orange-colored sandstone cliffs of his homeland. It always took him a while to settle into reality after suffering through a nightmare like that.

Walking into his superior's office, Hunter tried to shake the growing suspicion that his upcoming assignment would be life-changing.

"The shuttle bus driver was killed," said Captain Ernest Sam, his immediate supervisor for Tribal Criminal Investigations. "And four of the passengers were taken to the hospital at Farmington by air ambulance."

"Bad judgment, driving along that lonely stretch after midnight." Hunter had a lot of questions, but he wasn't about to ask them of Captain Sam, a man who could very well be one of the evil ones.

Hunter's biggest wish was to find a subtle way of keeping all strangers and other innocents off Navajoland roads at night. There was a secret war going on. A war that periodically broke out in disastrous skirmishes. Perhaps one exactly like this morning's bus wreck.

A criminal investigator for the Navajo Department of Public Safety, Hunter was also a warrior in the covert army of the Brotherhood, a group of medicine men who were fighting to free the land of a modern-day scourge of Navajo witches. This particular group of bad guys called themselves Skinwalkers, after the ancient legends of supernatural Navajo shape-shifters.

Hunter figured using the term had been a good call on their part. The People cringed at the very word, and refused to discuss anything about witchcraft with anyone, including their neighbors and the police.

Hunter owed his first allegiance to the noble Brotherhood during this troubled time. And Captain Sam was not one of them.

Hunter's gut instincts were telling him this bus crash was connected to Skinwalkers.

"We need you to go up there and take a look," the captain said. "There's bound to be lots of questions about the whole thing, and probably a ton of lawsuits. Best to have our answers ready before the accusations begin. Do a complete job, and do it right. I'm taking you off everything else for a few days."

Hunter nodded in agreement and turned to leave the captain's office.

"Be ready for a crowd at the accident site," Sam called after him. "I've heard the TV reporters are already arriving. And a contact called a few minutes ago from the executive director's office in Window Rock. Levi George himself is on his way to the crash site."

Shrugging, Hunter flipped on his hat and stepped out of the police station into the burgeoning heat of the early September morning. So old "Sarge" George, now the executive director of the Navajo Department of Public Safety, wanted to get his face in front of the cameras. Terrific. That meant most of the accident scene would be trampled and evidence destroyed for sure. There wouldn't be much left to investigate.

Hunter's cell phone vibrated in the breast pocket of his khaki uniform as he clicked open the driver's door on his 4X4 SUV. It was the two-buzz signal that meant someone in the Brotherhood was trying to reach him.

He flipped it open and held it to his ear.

"Wauneka." His cousin Ben, a medical doctor and also a member of the Brotherhood, announced himself. "I've been called to the Farmington hospital to assist in the treatment of the wounded bus passengers." He didn't bother to ask if Hunter knew about the accident. "One of the injured women came to consciousness a few minutes ago," he added. "She's claiming her daughter is missing."

"Daughter? How old?"

"Toddler. Almost a year. Thing is, no kids were accounted for on the bus. We don't have a complete passenger list yet, but no one under twenty has been found."

"You think her kid was thrown into the brush during the crash and hasn't been located?"

"No." The answer came quietly, with deadly implications. "The mother also claims another woman was holding her baby at the time of the crash. There's been no sign of the woman she describes, either."

"Then you believe the crash was some kind of Skinwalker attack or diversion? That the other woman perhaps was one of *them?* And on the bus just to get the child? Why would they take a baby?"

"We can make guesses forever. Find the little girl. That should give us some answers."

Hunter flipped off his phone then hopped into his SUV and cranked the engine. But he didn't turn onto the highway in the direction of the crash site. He had a few preparations to make first.

It looked as though he would be more than a simple police investigator this time. Tracking a woman and a child for the Brotherhood and potentially facing the Skinwalkers meant he had better get himself mentally and physically ready.

Being the best tracker in all the Western states was not nearly enough to save him from Skinwalker magic. There were sacred prayers and chants he had to start saying, in case the crash really was the work of the evil ones.

Though, in the end, there was no kind of magic that could hide them from him. He straightened his back and made another vow. The lost child would be returned to her mother, no matter how many Skinwalkers he had to track down to get the job done.

Bailey's mind began to clear. She felt as if she were swimming up to consciousness from a deep well of liquid fog. Somewhere in the background she could hear men's voices, loud and raspy. And then the growls of a snarling dog.

She tried to pry open at least one eye and focus. But as

a dim light penetrated her eyelid, the sudden bolt of pain in her head made it easy to decide to keep it closed. Her whole body hurt, but the horrible aching in her temples was nearly unbearable.

She chose to deal with the searing torment by shutting her mind down again. Never let it be said that Bailey Howard faced pain straight on. Not if she could avoid it.

And not when returning to sleep might bring back the dream she'd been having of that wonderful summer, staying with Anali and being young and in love.

Sweet memories surfaced in Bailey's half-asleep state. Memories of a time when she'd thought she had everything. She was thrilled to be back there, even if it was only a dream.

Out of the black depths, a new noise broke into her reverie. The harsh male voices were still there. But instead of the growling dog, this time she heard a baby's cries.

A baby? Suddenly everything came back in a whirl of motion and sound. There had been a crash. And she'd been holding a little girl when the lights went out.

Bailey's eyes blinked open and she found herself seated in the back seat of an open-topped Jeep. What the heck was she doing here? And where was baby Tara?

"It's about time you came around, pretty momma." The raspy male voice sounded uncomfortably close to her ear. "Your kid's making too much noise. You'd better shut her up. We're going to have to walk from here, and I don't like that whiny stuff."

"My…" She swallowed hard against her dry throat and turned her head toward the voice.

And immediately wished she hadn't. A wave of nausea kicked her in the gut as she got a whiff of foul breath from the dirty man, who was standing just outside her door. Turning her face away, she saw the baby on the other side of the back seat. The kid was tied into some kind of ratty carrier.

"Where's the baby's mother?" she mumbled as she tried to reach for Tara. A second later she realized her hands were pinned behind her back, and she couldn't get them free.

Forget the kid's mother, where the heck was *she?* And why were her hands tied?

"*You're* the baby's mother. Snap out of it and start making sense." The man grabbed her by one shoulder and dragged her out of the vehicle.

Bailey's knees crumpled under her. When the gruff man fisted his hands in her hair and brought her to her feet, it felt as if every strand was being pulled from her scalp. Then he shoved her hard against the bumper.

Seeing stars, she screamed at the rough treatment and kicked out at him.

"Shut up." He raised his hand and smacked her across the face. "We can carry your kid, but you gotta walk. And you have to be real quiet."

"Gag her and drug the kid again, Jacquez," another man said from behind the Jeep. "We need to get on up the hill now before the cops show up."

Tears welled in her eyes. "At least tell me why—"

Before she could finish the question, a cloth that smelled of gasoline was jammed into her mouth. Another wave of nausea hit her, but she fought it down. She was barely able to breath as it was; no sense choking on her own vomit.

The smelly guy named Jacquez left her leaning against the Jeep, and walked toward the baby. Panicked that he would hurt Tara, Bailey ran after him and tried to knock him off his feet with her body.

A pair of strong arms came from behind, grabbed her by the waist then threw her to the dirt. "You do what you're told, girlie. And no funny stuff."

Looking up at the other man, who was obviously Navajo and had the wildest eyes imaginable, she heard herself whimper. The guy called Jacquez might be smelly and mean, but this one seemed absolutely insane. Bailey was paralyzed with terror.

"Get to your feet." The crazed Indian bent down, grabbed hold of the front of her shirt and pulled her to a standing position.

She cried out at the pain. But as spots swam before her eyes, she was surprised how little sound got past the gag. Oh, God, she was going to suffocate and die.

Managing to steady herself and temporarily quiet her boiling hysteria, she tried backing away from the crazy man's reach. Maybe she could escape.

The devil pinched her nipples, rough and hard, before he let go. "You're a real pretty one. We gotta keep you alive, but I know ways to make you wish you were dead." He unsheathed a huge knife from his belt and pushed the tip toward her nose. "Be a terrible shame to mess up that face. You do what you're told and don't cause no trouble, and maybe you'll keep your skin."

Bailey sniffed back her panic and remembered to breathe through her nose. For a spilt second, she wondered if she wouldn't be better off dead. Why hadn't she died in that crash?

But then an image of getting even with these two for putting her through this hit her squarely between the eyes. And she got mad.

Mad enough to stay alive.

* * *

Dressed in desert camouflage gear so he wouldn't be spotted, Hunter stealthily circled around back of the crash site. The highway had been blocked off and TV cameramen, reporters and crime-scene technicians swarmed over the side of the ravine.

He stood in a shallow, dry creekbed in the shadow of a few sycamores and studied the scene through his binoculars. There were people everywhere, both on the road with the news vans and down the hill around the crash site.

A contingent from Director George's office, including the barrel-chested man himself, was giving interviews in front of the cameras. Inside the bus, a couple of investigators Hunter recognized as FBI staff were gathering evidence.

Waiting until he could positively identify all the FBI field agents, Hunter was pleased to discover his own brother was not among them. Pleased, because he needed a word with Kody in private.

Hunter hunkered down and punched the button on his cell phone that would reach Kody directly.

"Brother," Kody answered before the first ring was complete. "I have news. The child that's missing is a granddaughter of Willie Concho, the patriarch of the Water-Flows-Apart Clan."

Hunter whistled through his teeth. Willie Concho was a powerful man in the northern New Mexico section of the Four-Corners reservation. Land, politics and money made him a breed apart from most of the Navajos in Dinetah. He lived in a castle, with a real moat and a whole army of guards surrounding the place.

"Has there been a ransom demand?" Hunter asked.

"If so, the FBI has not been informed. We do have instructions to keep the disappearance under absolute wraps, though. There will be no Amber alert and no one is to mention the missing child. Publicity could get her killed in a hurry."

"Will the tribal police be informed?

"No, and…" After a split second's hesitation that no one but a member of the Brotherhood would've noticed, Kody continued, "…we have a positive identification on the missing woman."

"Someone we know," Hunter guessed.

"Bailey Howard, of the White Streak People in Many Cliffs."

"What?" A purple haze of memories colored Hunter's vision for a moment. "No way. She hasn't set foot in Dinetah in years. Last I heard she was working for her father's company in New York."

"We confirmed it with her dad a few minutes ago. She was coming back to pack up her grandmother Howard and transfer her to a nursing home in Albuquerque. The old woman's apparently in the first stages of Alzheimer's. But her clan has decided the grandmother is witched, so they've abandoned her in fear.

"And as panicked as he is about Bailey's disappearance," Kody added, "her father is still worried about publicity causing more harm than good. And he has a point. We've convinced him not to come to Dinetah yet. To let us try to handle it first."

Hunter took a breath. "It's a shame about the grandmother, and no wonder they were concerned. Not much a sick old lady can do to take care of herself without her clan to stand beside her."

It wasn't the Navajo Way to push the sick and old out

in the cold. But fear of witchcraft was strong among the rural Dine.

"Is it possible Bailey was kidnapped for ransom, too?" Hunter asked. "I saw her father's name on the Forbes richest Americans list."

"It's true Luther Howard has made much of his Anglo father-in-law's company over the years," Kody replied. "That is one smart city Navajo who managed to turn himself into a billionaire. But I seriously doubt Bailey was an intended victim. She supposedly had the baby on her lap and I'm guessing the kidnappers mistook her for the mom."

Sophisticated Bailey Howard holding a baby? Hunter found himself smiling at the perplexing image.

"The Howard family knows how to avoid unwanted publicity," Kody continued. "And it's a sure bet if the paparazzi got wind of her being on the reservation, it would make things a lot harder for the grandmother. And now it might mean Bailey's life, too."

Hunter waited for his brother to finish.

"Luther Howard said he would stay away on one condition. He asked specifically for your tracking services."

"I can't imagine that he even knows who I am."

"He knows Bailey was stuck on you in college," Kody said. "We all remember it quite well. I guess Mr. Howard has been keeping *track* of *you*."

"Who took them?" Hunter asked, not willing to dwell on the past. "Have we got any leads?"

"Nothing for sure. But one of the passengers with minor injuries talked about seeing a big dog and hearing a car engine start up right after the crash."

"A dog, not a wolf?"

"Definitely a dog," Kody told him. "The fellow swears

this one was a combination mastiff and Great Dane—but bigger and meaner. Scared the guy so badly he kept quiet and pretended he was out cold to avoid a confrontation with the animal."

"You're thinking Skinwalkers, aren't you?"

"It's likely. But we don't have enough information. I haven't heard rumors of a dog witch. Are you going after them now?"

"Should I wait for the FBI?"

Kody chuckled. "You know it will probably take the Bureau hours to notify their own trackers and mount a search party. It's going to be even harder, since Washington has decided to keep this under wraps. You start now and let us wait for the ransom demands. If this is Skinwalker business, the FBI won't be of much help, anyway.

"I'll keep trying to reach Lucas Tso so he can ask the Bird People for help," Kody added. "He's away from Dinetah at a gallery showing in Scottsdale.

"You keep in touch, brother. And be careful."

Sixty miles north of Hunter's location, the Navajo Wolf in his human form inspected renovations made to his cavern hideout. He'd picked this spot because of the difficulty in entering. The only way in and out, except for his newly excavated elevator shaft, was by river. Twenty miles from the nearest road and invisible from above, the cave was well hidden from law enforcement.

It was perfect for what he had in mind. And this spot had to be close to where the ancient parchments had been buried a thousand years ago. He could almost taste victory. The secrets of eternal life were very nearly his.

All he needed now was the map to find them.

"Excuse me, sir." One of his Skinwalker lieutenants broke into his thoughts. "We've received the newest advisories. The kidnapping has gone well. They are headed back through the roughest, most remote terrain. No one will be able to follow them there, and the child seems fine so far."

The Wolf brushed the man's words aside with a wave of his hand. "And the map? What happened with our covert action at the Concho ranch?"

His underling cowered behind a folding table covered with maps and papers. "That skirmish was not decided in our favor. The Rodent you sent wasn't able to gain access to the ranch. He claims the perimeters are protected with magic."

"The Brotherhood." Who else would know of ancient ways to slow down the Skinwalkers?

The lieutenant shrugged and the Wolf suffered a wave of nausea so strong he had to breathe deeply to keep from fainting. He had not been feeling well of late, and he needed those parchments to fix it. He had to get that damn map.

There was no choice now but to demand it as ransom for the child.

An hour later Hunter slowed his 4X4 at the crest of a mesa and took a sip of water from his canteen. Driving as fast as the stony, eroded terrain would allow, he'd been bouncing along on old sheep track, following the signs of a vehicle about two or three hours ahead.

He'd easily read the clues of what had occurred downhill from the crash site, without ever being seen by the dozens of onlookers who were still trampling evidence at the scene. Someone had gone to a lot of effort to erase the signs of footprints and Jeep tire treads, but hadn't counted on Hunter's ability to read the tracks.

He wasn't modest or proud about his talent, but he was sure no one within a thousand miles was as good a tracker as he was.

Hunter had found clear evidence, even in the hard-packed ground, that told of two men and a big animal with oversize dog prints who had dragged a woman away from the crash site. Judging by faint tire tracks, they'd put her into one of those ancient, open Jeeps like the back-country guides sometimes used.

The animal's prints had disappeared, as if it had flown away from the scene. But the others had gotten into the vehicle, which had been secreted behind one of the massive boulders at the base of the ravine. The Jeep and its occupants had left the hiding place several hours before he'd read the signs. Hunter deduced they'd been gone since dawn.

He noted, by the depth of boot heel prints that they had missed brushing from the sand, the taller of the two men had picked up an extra twenty pounds. It seemed like enough added weight to account for the baby.

If he was right about the time, they had about a three-hour head start. Even stopping every twenty minutes to get out and check the signs to be sure he was still on track, Hunter was continuing to gain on them.

They'd stopped every few miles themselves. The men had gotten out, brushed around their tire tracks and then hovered over something in the back seat. The baby was very likely slowing their progress.

Hang on, Bailey. I'm coming. Hazy images of a passion-filled summer entered his mind when Hunter should've been concentrating on the tracks. *Hang on, Bailey, I want to go with you.*

Damned images. He'd tried for years to forget them.

"Stay with me," he remembered urging her, back when the world was younger. And then he'd laughed as he moved his body faster and faster inside her waiting warmth, and watched her coming right along to the heights with him.

How young they both had been. How full of themselves, and how obsessed by tender lust for each other. Their affair had thrown him totally out of balance. It had taken him years to find harmony again.

He remembered her saying she loved him, but he wasn't positive Bailey had even known what the term meant. In his mind, he also had a vague memory of her saying how much she loved her newest discoveries of liquor and cigarettes. As spoiled as she had been, it was doubtful she could've loved anyone but herself.

He wondered how she might've changed during eight years.

Hunter gritted his teeth at the memories and set his jaw. It didn't matter. She and an innocent child were in real trouble, and he was the only one who could save them.

If this kidnapping was Skinwalker doing, they didn't stand a chance of losing their shadow with him on the trail. He doubted the Skinwalkers would understand that the Brotherhood was after them until it was too late. His cousins worked hard to keep their identities a secret from the evil ones.

The kidnappers might think they were so far ahead that no one could follow, but they hadn't counted on being tracked by Hunter Long instead of the FBI. Well, they would know soon enough.

Hang on, Bailey. I'm coming.

Chapter 2

Bailey would've given a year of her life for a drink of water and a bathroom stop. Come to think of it, she would dearly love to give up *this* year of her life.

Amazing. All she wanted was plain water. Imagine that. The counselors in rehab would be proud.

Her old friends—well, she couldn't really say they'd been all that friendly, more like conspirators in addiction—would've called her a wimp. But she was *way* over what any of them would think. She hadn't cared since the day she'd woken up alone and sick, and had signed herself in for treatment.

Now, her pedicured and pampered feet had blisters on every square inch. Who would've thought that a fabulous new pair of designer pumps could turn out to be her worst nightmare?

The two Navajo creeps who were dragging her and baby

Tara up and down rocky cliffs had at last taken the gag out of her mouth. There was no sense in screaming. Not out here, a zillion miles from civilization.

With arms aching from being tied, her stomach growling, and sweat leaking from every pore, Bailey had to bite her tongue to keep the panic from overtaking her. If she knew nothing else, it was clear these two Neanderthals would just as soon kill her as look at her. And the method of her death would not be pretty—or fast.

After giving it a little thought, she'd decided to let them continue to think she was Tara's mother. From what she'd overheard, they had deliberately searched for Tara at the bus crash. They'd known the baby's name and, unlike their disregard for Bailey's welfare, they seemed interested in keeping the kid in at least minimally decent physical shape as they climbed the cliffs.

Which wasn't so easy, since they'd been traveling through sand and around boulders in double time. One of the men had Tara's carrier tied on like a backpack. Every time the child cried, they stopped long enough to give her a bottle that apparently contained some kind of a sedative mixed with water.

Bailey could barely keep up with them. In fact, twice she'd gone down on her knees in the gravel and loose rocks. But the not-quite-human idiot on the other end of her rope never even slowed down as she scrambled back to her feet.

It was a damn good thing the counselors at rehab had insisted she exercise with a personal trainer. She was in the best physical shape of her life.

But that didn't mean her poor body wouldn't have bruises and cuts everywhere. Her new black suit was nearly ripped to shreds. And don't even get her started on the brand-new, fifty-dollar-a-pair, thigh-high nylons.

Mr. Smelly-guy Jacquez, who'd been dragging her by the rope, suddenly slowed and the line went slack, making Bailey look up. They had come to a solid wall of rock at the end of a steep canyon.

The man with the baby, who'd been leading the way, shifted the carrier around to his chest and inched through a slit in the rocks that Bailey hadn't even noticed. Without a word of warning, Mr. Smelly pulled her close and then pushed her ahead of him through the same small opening.

She found herself in a dark and shadowy place that was at least twenty degrees cooler than the desert floor where she'd been a second ago. When her eyes got used to the change in light, she saw they'd stepped into a cleft in the rocks and were heading for a natural rock staircase that rose straight up the side of a two-hundred-foot cliff.

"We're not climbing up there, are we?" she asked without thinking. "I can't with my hands tied. I'll fall."

"Quit whining, bitch," Jacquez said with a snicker that spewed slimy saliva all over her face. "When we get to the top, we're going to rest for a while. You'll get to put dry pants on your kid and make sure she's doing okay. And if you do a quick job of it, I might even give you a drink of water. Or something even more, uh, interesting, if there's time and you're a good girl."

"But…" Bailey bit her lip to keep quiet.

As angry and frustrated as she was, she knew complaining would only cause her more trouble. Dying from a fall was much preferable to dying by having your skin peeled off one piece at a time. She still wasn't entirely positive she wanted to live through the climb. What for?

Squeezing her eyes shut to stem the tears, she prayed that the police would be able to follow them through these wild surroundings. Certainly her father would've caused a huge fuss over her disappearance by now and made sure someone was trying to find her.

People must be coming for them. All she had to do was stay alive long enough for whoever it was to catch up.

It had taken all her dramatic abilities so far to pretend she was Tara's mother. Changing diapers had not been a big part of her previous social schedule. But doing it well enough to fool the goons had meant her and Tara's survival, so she'd muddled through.

She would keep on getting by, too, by God. But someone had better be right behind them, coming to the rescue. If they weren't, Bailey was positive it was only a matter of time before the entire show would be over and the curtain on her life would come down for good.

Hunter parked his SUV in a dry wash about a hundred yards behind the Jeep he'd been following. From his vantage point, it looked abandoned.

He'd been having second, third and fourth thoughts about the whereabouts of the dog. Was the mixed breed really a Skinwalker witch, and had it flown away from the crash site? Or was it a real dog that had somehow managed to get into the Jeep without him identifying the tracks?

A Skinwalker would be terrifying and difficult to confront. But Hunter had a few tricks up his sleeve when it came to these modern witches, thanks to the Brotherhood.

The possibility of it being a real mastiff-Great Dane mix had left him with a growing anxiety. He'd seen a good bloodhound catch a man's scent from two hundred yards away. And last week, in his job as police investigator, Hunter had been called to the scene of a wild dog attack on one of the People's herds.

Being in the midst of such savagery had made the reality of a dog attack stick with him. And made him more cautious than usual.

He checked the slender knife secreted inside his boot and the wide hunting blade sheathed on his belt. Both were sharp and within easy reach. Then he ran his hand under the seat until he came up with the sealed stash of skunk musk he carried with him at all times. It wouldn't take much of the stuff to throw a real dog off the scent.

Putting a drop or two on the backs of his hands so it wouldn't be close enough to his eyes to make them sting, Hunter was satisfied at the protection it afforded. He stepped out of the SUV and cautiously crept toward the Jeep. Every few feet he stopped and listened. Hearing nothing but the faint rustle of rodents scurrying to hide from the musky-smelling intruder in moccasin boots, he soon realized the men and their captives were long gone.

It didn't take more than a minute of inspecting the abandoned Jeep for him to decipher what had happened. Two men had driven here and parked the vehicle deliberately. There was no sign of the dog. The two had gotten out, removed several objects from the rear and then one of them had picked up the baby from the right back seat and walked away.

The other man had pulled Bailey bodily from the left side. Hunter saw the signs of a small struggle. And when he looked closer, he found a few drops of blood on the bumper. Bailey's? The clues seemed to suggest it.

His own blood heated. He began imagining ways to

inflict as much pain as possible on the two creeps when he caught up to them.

Squatting down with his face close to the ground, he soon deduced they'd gone toward one of the few sources of water to be found for miles around. It was a difficult trek and nearly impossible to execute unless you knew where to go.

Hunter wondered why they had decided to use that desolate and difficult area for a getaway. The choice didn't make any sense. All his Navajo training in order and balance made him search for answers when things refused to be reasonable. It was what made him a good cop.

But he would have to chew on the problem while he chased them down. It looked as if they still had about a two-hour lead.

He smiled when he thought how fortunate he was that they had chosen to run in the remote area that sprawled along the border between Utah and Arizona. Perhaps that was one of the reasons the kidnappers had made that particular decision. Most trackers would've needed hours of map reading and perhaps a native guide to know where to look for water holes.

But Hunter didn't need any maps. He'd spent many of his boyhood summers helping his mother's people tend their sheep herds among these canyons and sandstone slabs. He would have little trouble following the men, even across natural rock formations and among boulders that normally left no useful signs for a tracker.

What's more, it looked as if they were having to drag Bailey behind them. Good girl. Not that he liked thinking of her being treated that way, but she was slowing them down. Giving him a chance to catch up.

Hurrying back to his SUV, he stuffed the canteen in his lightweight backpack. Then he checked his ammunition belt, threw it over his neck and picked up the carbine. He would be traveling light, but he would be traveling prepared.

As a last-minute thought, he took his cell phone out of his breast pocket and plugged it into a portable battery pack he always carried in the SUV. Then he crammed the plastic jar with the skunk musk into his pocket. No cell phone reception where he was headed.

None of it was making much sense to him yet. But he was damn sure not going to risk being unprepared. Not when it might mean the lives of two people.

And not when one of them was the only woman he might ever have loved.

Bailey was too scared to sleep. Mr. Smelly had been true to his word and gave her one lone sip of water after she'd changed Tara's diaper. Then he'd ordered her to get some sleep, saying they would be here for only a half hour or so. He expected her to keep up.

The climb up the rock cliff had been terrifying. Her leather pumps were all wrong for navigating slippery surfaces.

Fortunately, Mr. Smelly had not dragged her up here. If he had, she probably would've fallen to her death for sure. Instead, he'd left her wrists tied but had shoved her up the steps ahead of him. Anytime she hesitated, fighting to get her footing on the slick rocks, the bastard had reached up and pinched her bottom hard to make her go faster.

The bruises might prove to be permanent.

She was hot, hungry and hurting all over. But most of all, she'd begun to really worry about the baby. The little girl had been listless and limp this time when she'd changed her. Bailey wasn't positive how long it had been since the bus crash, because her watch had been smashed.

But the poor kid must not have had anything to eat in at least eighteen hours.

"I said sleep," Mr. Smelly yelled. He took a threatening step in her direction and she closed her eyes.

What were they going to do with tiny Tara? Bailey wasn't sure the baby would last much longer without some real food.

For that matter, what were they going to do with her? The rhetorical question had way too many excruciating possibilities for her to contemplate.

She took a deep breath, felt the pain in all parts of her body and fell sound asleep.

Sunshine beat down on her face as she stretched lazily in the noonday heat. Hunter faced her, sitting crossed-legged on the wide, flat rock and grinning at her while she made erotic sounds of contentment. Below them, in a crystal pool carved by nature from ancient sandstone, a thousand points of reflected sunlight glittered in a joyful dance.

"You look very smug, Miss Howard," he said, sounding sure of himself.

His long chestnut hair lay in wet strands across his shoulders, allowing tiny droplets of water to slither down his muscled chest and follow their own path to lower regions. Regions where Bailey's fingers were dying to follow.

A couple of young idiots, both of them were still stark naked after their skinny-dip in the remote freshwater pond.

She refused to stop herself from doing whatever felt best in the moment. Why not? Who would get hurt?

Reaching over, she ran her hand in light circles up his thigh. "You look pretty contented yourself, Hunter Long."

His slate-gray eyes grew dark with passion. She loved it when they did that—turned to steel as he looked at her body. In fact, she loved pretty much everything about her Native American lover.

Bailey had never thought of herself in quite those terms before she'd come to stay with her Navajo grandmother for the summer. But in truth, both she and Hunter were half-breeds.

Her with deep brown hair, golden skin and mixed up hazel eyes. Hunter with his lighter hair, worn long in warrior style, and his tuxedo-gray eyes that made him look more like a beachboy surfer dude than a descendant of the first Americans.

They made a great pair. And great lovers.

Hunter leaned over and stroked her earlobe with the tip of his tongue. Fire burned where he lathed the outline of her ear, sizzling down her spine to her core and igniting that special spot between her legs.

Oh, the man could do such wonderful things to her…and with her.

At first, she'd been surprised that such a strong, athletic male could be so tender a lover. But soon she'd become addicted to the sensual strokes of his tongue and the long, smooth way he glided his fingers across the sensitive parts of her body.

"Invite me to come inside and play, beauty," he whispered against her lips.

Her laugh erupted, giddy and high-pitched in anticipation. "I thought I already did."

Come inside, my love, she begged him with her eyes. You are much more than simply invited. You are welcome here anytime.

* * *

"You waiting for an engraved invitation, bitch?" A harsh voice matched the rough fingers that were digging into her shoulder and bringing her out of her slumber with a crash. "I told you to get up. You've got thirty seconds to get to your feet and get that kid's diaper changed again. We're moving out and I don't plan on leaving any stragglers behind—not alive, anyway."

Bailey cringed. Reality was such a cold shock after the sweet dreams of making love with Hunter that her eyes filled with tears she dared not shed.

She gritted her teeth and did what she was told. But all the while, she couldn't help but think of her long-lost lover and wish he were here.

He never lost his temper or acted moody. Calm, charming and so incredibly tender it made her cry sometimes, he was everything these creeps were not.

In fact, his cool detachment and Cheshire-cat smile were what had driven her to leave him in the end. Hard to imagine it right now, but he was *too* even-tempered and in control. So much so that Bailey never knew what he was thinking, or what he wanted past the great sex.

He had asked her to let him come inside and play. But he had never opened up and given her a glimpse of what made him tick. Nor had he ever committed himself. She had told him she loved him, but he had never returned the sentiment. It had been so frustrating.

Idly wondering if he was still single, she handed a cleaned-up Tara over to their captors and then held out her hands so they could be bound together once again. Bailey had hoped to casually run into Hunter while she was on the reservation. Simply to see how he was doing after all this time, of course.

The young Hunter Long had made it quite clear that she
didn't have enough of a Navajo temperament to suit him. Had
he found a Dine woman to marry? Her curiosity was piqued.

But her chances of running into *anybody* ever again
seemed to grow slimmer and slimmer with every hour.
Was she destined to get out of this mess alive? Perhaps not,
but she wasn't ready to die. Not yet. She wasn't even ready
to start praying, she was still so angry.

She didn't need charming Hunter Long at the moment.
What she needed was a big, mean policeman. And, please
God, make him arrive soon.

Hunter followed a broken shale path as it snaked
through a dry arroyo. Tracking here required the ultimate
care and skill. Except for a couple of small detours, the kidnappers seemed to be heading straight toward the one
freshwater source.

Odd how they didn't seem too worried about being
followed anymore. Perhaps they figured no one could keep
up with the pace they had set.

Hunter took a minute to climb one of the granite out-
croppings in his path. From the top of the rock that had
been worn smooth by millions of years of wind and rain,
the sun's rays were still visible in the reddish glow of the
western sky.

Off to the southwest, one of the vast black cloud formations that sometimes built to thousands of feet high during the
late summer appeared to threaten rain. As dry as it had been
this year, he knew the promise of healing water wouldn't
come to fruition. In a few minutes the sun would disappear,
cooling the earth and dissipating the thunderclouds.

Perhaps in another few weeks the Navajos' next-door

neighbors, the Hopis, would begin their rain ceremonies, and then the clouds would grant their healing blessings on both tribes' land. The Hopis could call the clouds. It was part of their supernatural beliefs and sacred ceremonies.

Hunter leaned back against the granite shelf and turned his face to a cool breeze brought on by the clouds and the growing dusk. Taking a second to admire the contrast of towering gray-and-tan thunderheads to the navy-blue skies of sunset was a big part of the Navajo Way of restoring harmony and limiting stress.

The Hopis could call on their gods for rain. The Navajos would enjoy the beauty of it.

Another stray breeze, from the north this time, brought the smell of water. He inched around to face the distant Utah border, and realized he had reached a point where he could take a shortcut to the water hole.

If the kidnappers chose to stop there and rest, it would be a good spot for him to sneak into their camp and judge the difficulty of the situation. Did they keep their hostages tied at all times? And were the two victims kept together or separate during rest periods?

They hadn't taken any extended breaks during their trek so far. A few minutes to hide their tracks and change the baby was all they'd allowed themselves. Hunter had found the diapers buried in shallow pits. He was hopeful that the goons themselves would soon require a few hours' sleep before they continued toward their destination.

Which was where, exactly? he wondered.

Climbing down the other side of the granite spire, Hunter decided to quit tracking for the day. Instead he would make his way up the cliffs and over the mesas, and arrive at the watering hole within an hour. Getting there while they were resting and maybe sleeping was his best hope of catching them off guard.

Just before midnight, Hunter climbed down from the rocky cliffside path on Casa del Eco Mesa. It was a moonless night, so he used the infrared binoculars to scour the rocky oasis below him for any signs of life.

Watching a young coyote dip his head to take a drink, Hunter amended that to any sign of *human* life. He found nothing through his glasses except normal nocturnal desert creatures.

Had he missed the kidnappers? They had to have been headed in this direction. Was he too late? Or too early?

He squatted down, took a sip from his canteen and listened to the sounds of the night. He let his Navajo senses rule his thoughts. Who were these two men?

They had been moving fairly quickly up to now. Was that because they knew the area? Or because they had been told the way to go?

Using instinct and his best judgment, Hunter decided the two men he'd been following had not designed this elaborate kidnapping plan. A few of the things they had done left him positive they were not the brains of the operation, and that these muscle-for-hire dudes were not familiar with the terrain. They had probably stopped to read their maps earlier in the evening. Halting a few miles before reaching a natural rest stop like the water hole was not something a person familiar with the area would do.

That conclusion decided his next course of action. He would scout out a good hiding place and wait for them to arrive.

Hunter was known throughout the reservation for his

limitless patience. Bailey hadn't always appreciated that fact about him, he remembered.

But that was who he was. How he was raised. Unlike his older brother, Kody, who had been away at boarding school, Hunter had been in grade school when their father retired from being a master of disguises for the U.S. Marshal service in order to work as a consultant to the Navajo Tribal Police. Being only one-eighth Navajo, their old man had dragged Hunter from one small subagency office to the next, using him to translate from Navajo to English.

Hours of waiting, sometimes days of traveling in the car while trying to teach his father the Navajo language, had taught Hunter the value of patience. Though he'd had to fight within himself every day to maintain his Navajo sense of balance and harmony.

At the same time, he'd also learned a few things about his dad that he would've rather not known.

Hunter still had a lot of anger toward his father. And no way to let it loose, since the man had been dead for over ten years. But Hunter did know how to channel all that anger to good purpose when necessary.

It didn't matter how long he had to wait at the water hole for the kidnappers to show up. He would be ready to greet them when they arrived.

He had made up his mind that this was as far as they'd get. One way or another, Hunter planned to take their captives with him when he left.

It was only a matter of which of them had the most patience and whose will would be stronger. And in that kind of battle, he was unbeatable.

Chapter 3

Once again, Bailey stumbled to her knees on the hard gravel. "Hey," she shrieked.

"Shut up and stay put," Mr. Smelly Jacquez said as he kicked his foot in her direction. "We're stopping here. Don't make me punish you for talking."

She dropped back on her bottom and bit her lip so she wouldn't cry out against all the pains in her body. Inching her way by the light of the stars to the shadow cast by a boulder, she leaned her back against the rock and tried to focus on the actions of the two creeps. Hopefully, if she was out of sight, they would ignore her for a while.

It seemed odd that they were stopping again so soon. She hadn't heard Tara crying, so why the need to halt their march?

A scent of wetness reached her parched nose and throat. They must be near water. She was actually smelling water like an animal, for heaven's sake.

Bailey tried to swallow against the dryness in her mouth and ended up coughing. *No.* Please don't let them notice her.

A flashlight clicked on suddenly, terrifying her. Then she saw in the luminous glow that both her captors were only interested in the water. The man with the crazy eyes roughly dropped Tara's carrier from his back to a rock right next to a small black pool, but he kept one hand on the baby as he knelt to drink. Mr. Smelly was carrying the flashlight, and he trained the beam on the water, apparently trying to assure himself that it was drinkable.

Bailey wished they'd ordered her to take care of the baby while they were stopped. It was hell not knowing how Tara was getting along. How much farther would they be traveling like this? And how much more sedation could the poor child endure?

A few seconds later, both men were splashing water over themselves and laughing. Across the breeze she heard them talking to each other. The guy with the crazy eyes talked only in Navajo. Jacquez spoke English.

Bailey remembered a few words of her childhood Navajo, but it was difficult keeping up with their conversation.

"Only a couple more hours from here, and we're supposed to wait for daylight." She'd caught only the tail end of Mr. Smelly's words. "You sure we have to keep the woman alive until we get there? Dragging her is a pain in the ass."

The response in Navajo was not totally clear. But what she did understand sent a chill down her spine.

"And orders are to keep the kid healthy until we get to the cabin. Some old wet-nurse has been hired to meet up with us there and she'll take care of the brat until the baby's grandfather pays up."

"Then we will kill the mother?"

The man with the wild look in his eyes laughed again. "When we get to the cabin, we can do whatever we like with the mother. Maybe there will be some fun to be had before we get rid of her."

Bailey again didn't comprehend all the Navajo words, but found the sentiments unmistakable.

She had a few hours left and then…

Desperate, she fought with her numb brain to figure out a plan to avoid her fate. There didn't seem to be any way to physically break free from the two creeps before they got to their meeting place.

For a fleeting second, her only thought was of getting her hands on one more line of coke. Wouldn't drugs make this whole nightmare more bearable? Wouldn't it give her the strength to see it through?

With another blink of her too-dry eyelids, she came back to the horrible present with a deadly reality check. She knew drugs only complicated things. She'd at least learned that much in rehab. Besides, her parents would be terribly disappointed if she fell right back into her old habits.

Nope. She couldn't wish for that. When her father came to rescue her, Bailey intended for him to be proud of how she'd survived. And she would survive. She knew it.

Maybe if she offered the crazy goons money, they would let her go. Perhaps she could tell them who she really was, give them her father's name and let them demand a ransom from him.

Why was Tara the one who was so important for ransom, and not the baby's mother? It was confusing, but Bailey figured if the point was money, her father could no doubt match or best the baby's grandfather's fortune.

Luther Howard could easily pay for the release of both captives. No problem.

It wasn't much, but it was the only plan she could come up with when her whole being throbbed in pain and her brain had shut down due to exhaustion.

She felt a sob well up in her chest. But there were no more tears left in her dehydrated body.

Oh, please send someone to save her and Tara, she prayed. She couldn't let herself imagine that this would be her end. Perhaps she should try bargaining with God for her life. She wasn't ready to die.

From his hiding place, Hunter could hear the two men's conversation. And he knew Bailey must hear it, too. Did she understand the Navajo words? It didn't matter much. He was positive she understood their meaning.

Even in the dark he was impressed by how calm she looked. Safely hidden behind a creosote bush within twenty feet of her, he let his eyes devour her image. It had been eight long years, but his body reacted to her nearness the same way it always had.

Though what he'd first thought he'd seen was really his memory. He looked again. Bailey's very real cuts and bruises were evident even without the infrared glasses. The skirt and jacket she wore were hanging on her frame by mere threads. She had been abused and probably starved, but his mind had refused to accept the current vision of his long-ago lover.

Over the years he had seen a few pictures of her in magazines and newspapers. So he wasn't surprised by the different cut of her hair. Still, he couldn't stop remembering how he had wrapped her long brunette curls around his fingers. Of how the silken strands would lie across his chest when they made love, and of how sensual and inviting they'd felt gliding against his belly in the heat of passion.

He shook his head and chided himself. This was no time to dream of the past. Bailey had made it clear when she left that their relationship was over for good.

It had been for the best, actually. Hunter had been too young then to comprehend how to keep himself in balance and still have all those erotic and chaotic feelings about her. But never again. He was a much tougher man today. The Skinwalkers were throwing the whole of Dinetah out of harmony, and yet most of the time he still managed to find peace within himself.

Back in the present, Hunter needed to focus so he could figure out the best way to get Bailey and the baby away. He thought for a second of killing both men. As a sworn officer of the law, he had the authority to use deadly force. That would certainly be one way to avenge their savagery.

But there were a few very good reasons not to kill them that he had better consider before he did anything rash. The first of those was the dark, moonless night. Though he had brought his infrared binoculars, the rifle was not equipped with a night scope.

He'd been watching the two men for a while, and the Navajo with the wild eyes never completely took his hands off the baby. No matter what else he did, that man obviously intended to deliver his precious package or die trying. If Hunter did manage to take him out while keeping the infant alive, he knew the other guy would get to the baby before he could take a second shot.

Unfortunately, that meant that killing both men in the

dark would very probably endanger the child's life more than was acceptable.

Then there was the possibility that their bosses were Skinwalkers. It seemed highly unlikely that these two were anything but hired help.

If Hunter killed them and then had to walk both an injured Bailey and the baby back out of the wilderness, he would be leaving them all open to attack. Skinwalkers would find them with no trouble and he would be hard-pressed to defend the two victims by himself.

He watched for a couple more minutes as the first man urged the baby to drink a few sips of water. Then both guys sat down to share rations they'd taken from a beat-up pack one of them had been carrying. They ignored Bailey, who was about fifty feet away and starting to nod off.

Would these two also take a nap? They didn't seem interested in whether Bailey got away or not. The main target of this kidnapping was obviously the baby. They must not know who the other hostage really was.

Hunter sat back on his heels and considered all the options. Taking both victims seemed impossible to do safely, presuming he could even manage to kill both men. He wasn't sure exactly where they were headed, but one had said it was only a few more hours away. Did Hunter dare take Bailey all the way out to civilization and leave the baby until he could come back?

If it were just him, he could climb the cliffs and mesas out of here and be back to his SUV in a few short hours. But he seriously doubted that Bailey was healthy enough to make the trip so fast.

While he continued to watch and consider, the men quieted and both seemed to fall asleep, the one curling himself around the baby's carrier. The time to make a decision was at hand.

Bailey tried not to fall asleep, though her body was screaming for rest. She wanted to keep watching the two creeps, and was petrified of never waking up.

Or, God forbid, Mr. Smelly Jacquez would decide he'd grown weary of her and simply walk away, leaving her behind. She wouldn't stand a chance out here in the wilderness, all alone with her hands tied.

As long as she was alive, there was an opportunity to buy her freedom. So the minute she saw them begin to gather their things to finish the journey, she intended to start negotiating for her life.

But she was so tired. And she was so damn cold. When the sun went down, the temperature dropped a few degrees every hour. It must now be thirty degrees colder than it was during the day.

Pulling her knees up, she tried to roll into a ball to stay warm. But the effort completely exhausted her. She couldn't keep her eyes open a minute longer.

A few seconds, or maybe an hour later, she awoke to find something warm and smelly pressing against her mouth. The shock startled her so badly her eyes popped open and she tried to scream. But whatever or whoever it was kept her quiet.

"Shush, beauty," a vaguely familiar voice whispered in her ear. "Let's try not to wake the two charmers, okay?"

Hunter Long? No, that was impossible. But she'd always been sure she would recognize his voice anywhere. She'd heard it in her dreams often enough. Was she dreaming?

Another shaft of panic hit her between the shoulder

blades. Who was this person? Someone coming to her rescue? Or another nightmare she would have to escape?

Trying to turn around to check, Bailey found herself firmly restrained by two strong arms.

"You ready to blow this picnic?" His casual tone and the slow drawl from behind her back reminded her only too well of easier, happier times. But her heart still threatened to pound right out of her chest.

"Nod your head if you can stand on your own."

Still stunned, Bailey managed only a shoulder shrug. She wasn't sure of anything right now except that it suddenly seemed she might make it out of this ordeal alive, after all. It was really Hunter. But how? Why?

"Okay, don't try," he murmured against her ear. "I'll carry you into the cliffs first. Far enough that the idiots can't follow. Relax and don't make a sound."

He released her mouth. Before she knew what was happening, Hunter had whisked her up in his arms and they seemed to be flying through the dark night.

She would've loved to be able to throw her arms around his neck and hang on, to enjoy the feel of his muscled chest after so many years. But her hands were still tied and she wasn't sure she had the energy left, anyway.

It seemed to take a long time, but probably it was only a few minutes that Hunter climbed among the boulders with her in his arms. Finally he reached a strip of level ground and halted.

"This is far enough. I'm going to set you down now, Bailey. Lean against me until you're steady. I'll cut the rope off your wrists in a second, but we still have to be quiet. Sound echoes in these canyons."

He slowly lowered her body along the length of his. Her

blistered and bloody feet rebelled with excruciating pain when they touched the ground, but she found a reserve of strength and ignored it. Leaning back against him, she silently kicked out the leg cramps until she could stand firmly upright and steady once again.

"Good girl. Now hold still while I cut the rope."

As the bonds went slack, she moved her arms apart. Without warning, sharp pains replaced the numbness in her fingers and nearly brought her to her knees. Whimpering, she pulled her throbbing hands to her chest.

The stabbing pain must've been clear on her face even in the darkness, because Hunter began vigorously rubbing her hands and forearms. "I know it hurts," he said soothingly. "But it'll go away in a moment."

He was right. A few minutes later the ache was a memory. She looked up into his face, wishing for tears enough to cry for joy.

Opening her mouth to thank him for saving her, she was surprised when he gripped the back of her head and covered her mouth in a searing kiss. It was all too short-lived, and a second later he pulled back. But he continued to grip her shoulders as if he was afraid she would fall down if he didn't. Or maybe that he would collapse if he had to let her go.

"Hunter..." She managed a dry, raspy squeak.

"Sorry," he said with a shake of his head. "But I'm so damn glad you're still alive. Forget it and have some water." He unscrewed the top from a canteen and handed it to her, then took it back after she'd had just a few gulps. "Not too much at one time, though. If it settles all right, you can try one of the MREs I'm carrying before we head off."

She cleared her less-parched throat and let her thoughts babble out. "Sheesh, your hands stink. Do you have any chocolate on you? What are you doing here?" She wasn't making sense, she knew. But she was so stunned her old lover had been the one to come to her rescue. "I demand to know if my father sent you or if this is as much a surprise to you as it is to me."

Even in the darkness of a moonless night, she could see his same old charming grin. The one she'd remembered through eight long years. Hunter had always been famous for flashing that boyish charm at all the girls.

"You haven't changed a bit, Bailey. Still the spoiled little rich girl, ordering everyone around. As it happens, your father did ask that I be the one to bring you home."

It was too much. She felt the weakness creeping up on her again. "Can I sit down? Please?"

"Sure. Here, let me help." The tone of his voice softened, evened out, ended up right back at that sexy baritone he'd always used to get into her pants when they were in college.

Once she was seated on the rocky shelf of a flat boulder, she began to feel stronger again. "So, why did he want you to come for me?"

Hunter chuckled in the darkness and she wished she could see his expression clearly. "I'm a Navajo Tribal Police special investigator. The best tracker west of the Mississippi."

"A cop? You sound like a character in an old black-and-white western." But unfortunately, everything about this whole horrible situation felt like a melodrama. Why shouldn't the dialogue be tacky, too?

Suddenly her stomach complained about her not eating in who knew how long. "You didn't say anything about chocolate. But you did mention MREs," she said. "I'm guessing that's something to eat."

"Army traveling food. Meals Ready to Eat. Not good, but filling." He handed her the canteen again. "Slowly."

A couple more sips of water and Bailey figured she was getting a second wind. Not having any chocolate to stem the desire to do a line was a disappointment, but she'd manage to get around the jitters with food instead.

"Does it take long to fix one of those MRE things?"

He shook his head and reached behind him to the pack on his back. "That's the whole point."

"Good. While I eat it, you can go back for the baby."

Shaking his head again, he ripped open the package and handed it to her. "I can't figure out how to manage taking both of you to safety at one time, Bailey. I have to get you out first and then come back."

"What? No. What will happen to Tara?"

"I can move fast. Depending on how bad your injuries are, I should be able to return before nightfall tomorrow. They want to keep the baby alive for ransom," he added. "She should be okay. As soon as you're safe, I'll come back for her."

"No." Bailey surprised herself by how adamant and full of strength her voice suddenly sounded.

"No?"

"We can't leave her with them. I can't believe I'm saying this, but please help me find a way to rescue her. I can't stand the thought of her being with them alone."

She waved a hand and her chin trembled. "I couldn't bear it if I live and Tara dies. Please, don't make me go."

* * *

Hunter leaned against the granite wall and stared out at a blanket of stars blazing in indigo skies. Without thinking, he reached down and stroked the silky rich hair of the woman whose head lay in his lap as she slept.

Bailey had been so exhausted that she'd nearly freaked out when he'd told her his plan to leave the baby behind. He'd come to a quick conclusion that her need for sleep was more acute than his need to whisk her away to safety.

They were temporarily not in danger, anyway, not up here on the shelf of this ancient sandstone monolith, with her tormentors sound asleep below them. So he intended to let her get as much healing sleep as possible before they started back toward civilization.

When she awoke, he hoped she would be in a more reasonable mood. It wasn't like the person he remembered to get so carried away with someone else's welfare—even if that someone else was a helpless child. Where had the selfish, spoiled Bailey Howard of his yesterdays gone?

The clear, high-desert night meant starlight illuminated most of their surroundings. Hunter had seen enough of Bailey's bruises and cuts to feel anger, strong and dangerous, well up from some dark place in his gut.

He hadn't liked the intense feelings all that much, and was glad there was a need to take Bailey back before he had to deal with the kidnappers. A few hours to calm down and regain harmony would definitely be a good thing.

The familiar flashback to his childhood and the terrible face of anger that was his clearest memory of his father came into his mind and set his teeth on edge. He had to fight it. Had to keep that awful genetic atrocity of memory tied down somewhere deep and hidden from view.

That exact same terror dwelled inside him, he knew. It ran in his blood, but he didn't have to give it free rein.

Hunter was a better man. He was good enough to know his limitations and he was Navajo enough to keep his spirit in balance.

He tried thinking of something else, and a picture of Bailey on their first date slipped into his head without warning. It had been on another late summer day, nearly ten years ago now.

But the skies were cerulean on that particular afternoon, the clouds tall and the same flint hue as the bluffs of his homeland. He'd suggested a picnic at his favorite place, high above Dinetah on a butte surrounded by aspen and spruce. The view was startling from up there and he'd wanted to impress her.

And he supposed he had. She'd turned her face to his in guileless wonder, her golden-amber eyes dancing with delight. "You must be able to see all the way to Colorado from here. It's beautiful," she'd murmured.

But he was the one to be impressed. He'd been rendered speechless. She was so beautiful she'd taken his words away—in two languages.

Bailey moaned and stirred in his lap, bringing him back to the present with a thud.

She pushed herself up. "How long have I been out?"

"A few hours." He reached for the canteen. "Have a little more water. Then maybe you can catch another hour or two of sleep before daybreak. I don't think we need to worry about getting too big a head start on your buddies, dumb and dumber. I'm willing to bet they won't be all that concerned about where you've gone."

She swallowed the water and took a deep breath. "Hunter…"

He wondered if she was trying to think of a way to thank him for coming to her rescue. That didn't sound much like the old Bailey Howard, and he would prefer she skip the accolades until they were really safe. But if she felt the need, he would sit quietly until she was finished.

"What can I say to make you understand that I can't leave Tara?" Bailey said, instead of the words he'd expected to hear. "Every second she's with those bastards the baby is in terrible danger. I couldn't live with myself if we left and she was injured—or worse. Please. If we can't get to her right away, can't we at least stay close by?"

It took him a second to catch up.

"Now, beauty," he began patiently. "I tried to explain this to you earlier. You're in no shape to be chasing around the desert after a couple of goons who are set on killing you. It's selfish for you to even consider it."

"Selfish?" When her argument hadn't gotten the response she'd obviously hoped for, Bailey tried a different tack. "You can help me. Teach me as we go. Show me how to follow along until we find a way to get her free. Please."

"No. It would be a stupid move."

Her next deep sigh carried a hint of anger. "You're being mean. Trying to get even with me for our breakup. That was *years* ago, Hunter. Get over it."

Ah. So now she was going to try using their old relationship to get what she wanted. That sounded a lot more like the girl he remembered.

"Bailey…" He let his tone of voice warn her that his mind was made up.

"Damn you," she whined. "This is really important. For the first time something is…" She stopped talking and he could tell the words had surprised her. He knew they'd shocked him.

"Look," she began again. "Not too many people know about this, but I recently finished five months in drug rehab."

He didn't let his surprise show in his face, The truth was, he wasn't sure how he felt about her revelation.

She hesitated for a second, then continued, "Part of the treatment consisted of being able to prioritize the things that are important. I found out something interesting. For me, nothing has ever been important until now. I was using drugs to cover up my meaningless existence."

"Hmm. Sounds like a bored little rich girl to me."

He felt her stiffen beside him. "There's that anger directed at me again. Damnit, Hunter, you're the one being selfish. Don't let your ancient hate for me cost Tara her life. That attitude isn't coming from the person I thought I knew years ago. Have you changed so much?"

"You don't know what you're talking about." He ground out the words. "I don't hate you. Far from it. But what you're asking would be foolish. I'm a lawman now. I have to consider every move responsibly.

"I've thought of what's best for the baby," he added. "But I have to do what's best for everyone. They won't hurt her. She's worth something special to them. Do as I say—"

His thought was interrupted by shouts coming from far below them. Apparently the kidnappers had discovered Bailey was missing, and were not particularly amused.

"The goony brothers are awake," he told her, letting the familiar grin color his tone. "I'm going to climb down and eavesdrop to see if they intend to search for you. Stay put and rest a few more minutes."

"But…"

"It has to be my way. Rest up. It's a long way back."

Hunter slipped off into the darkness. He'd need all that time to process the changes in Bailey.

Because every damn second he was with her seemed to be throwing him further and further out of balance.

Chapter 4

By the time Hunter crept close enough to catch the words of the two kidnappers, they were packing up to leave. He crouched beside a boulder and used the infrared glasses to study them as they argued with each other.

"Damned bitch!" the least crazy of the two growled at the other. "I hope she dies a slow miserable death. What kind of mother would leave her own kid?"

"You're only pissed 'cause you won't get a piece of that candy. Shut up and get the pack. Forget her. We're outta here."

"In the dark?"

Whining didn't seem to be getting the man too far. His insane buddy totally ignored him and reached for the baby carrier. But as he jerked it up off the ground, the surprised child awoke and shrieked in terror.

"Quiet!" the guy screamed at the baby. Roughly

shaking the carrier, he put his hand over the baby's mouth to muffle her cries.

Hunter was on his feet in an instant. He picked up the carbine and tried to get a bead on the man's head. One decent shot, that's all he needed.

But without the binoculars, he couldn't see well enough in the dark to pull it off. He might kill the child. Frustrated as hell, Hunter put down the rifle and counted to ten. But the goon's time on earth was running short. Daylight was only an hour or two away, and when Hunter caught up to him, the creep's existence in this world would be ended.

"Don't screw up the deal," the first man shouted at the insane one. "Give the kid another swig of those meds. Don't kill her."

Cussing under his breath, the man with the baby carrier reached for the pack and withdrew a bottle. He shoved it into the baby's mouth and let her take some of the liquid. In seconds, the child settled down. Then the man handed the bottle over to his comrade, jammed the baby's carrier onto his back and stalked out of the clearing.

"Wait up, damn it. I can't see you. It's dark as hell." The other man wasted little time following his buddy.

Hunter took a couple deep breaths. His plans had now changed. There was no way he would leave the child with those two creeps.

So, Miss Selfish Bailey Howard, get ready. You are about to have it your way.

Bailey came awake with a jolt. "Hunter?" He was leaning over her, and she could see his face clearly in the starlight. "You're back. Please, listen. Let me beg you one more time for—"

"Skip it," he told her with one of his too charming grins. "We're going after them at daybreak."

She sat straight up with her back against the wall. "What made you change your mind?"

Hunter knelt close and leaned on his heels. "Let's say I've decided to see how strong you really are. But you'd better not hold me back. And I don't want to hear a word of complaint about how much it hurts."

Nodding her head with a sharp promise, she agreed. "I swear. I won't say a word. Can we go now?"

"We need the light to follow their tracks. And we can use the next hour to get your feet ready to travel."

"My...?"

He leaned over and pulled off her shoes. "Your feet."

"Ouch." She hadn't realized how much it would hurt when the shoes were removed. How would she ever manage to put them back on?

She reached out to rub her toes but the skin hurt too much to touch. "Give me a second."

"You have to be able to walk to keep up with me. This was your idea. But if you can't..."

"My feet will be fine. I'm tougher than I look."

"Sure you are. Right."

"Look, bring it on. I am woman. I can walk ten miles in the city in stilettos. A few minor blisters aren't going to slow me down."

"Can you stand on them at all?"

"Maybe."

"Try it now." He stood, crossed his arms and waited.

Holding on to the solid rock behind her, Bailey put her stocking-clad feet under her and inched her way to a standing position. She grimaced at the shooting pains, but kept her mouth firmly closed.

"Okay, good enough," he said. "I'm going to carry you down to the water hole. I saw a couple of things there that will help." He swung her up in his arms and headed off, moving slowly down the jagged cliffs.

For a second she was stunned speechless. The flashing burn of heat as his body came in contact with hers made all the hairs on her skin stand up and crackle.

"Put me on my own feet," she said through gritted teeth. "I can go by myself. I said I wouldn't hold you back."

"Quiet," he whispered roughly. "The goons aren't too far away yet. Voices carry out here. Stay still. We'll be there in a few minutes."

This time, the flash of heat was pure, unadulterated anger. Damn him, anyway. Who did he think he was?

The answer came, loud and clear. *The man who is saving your life and helping to rescue Tara, you idiot.*

Yes, well…

Bailey clamped her mouth and her eyes shut. Everything was exactly the way she remembered it from those distant summers. Hunter did whatever he wanted and said very little in the meantime. In the past, he'd always gotten his way with a smile and fast moves, and apparently he still did.

It was more frustrating than ever. She wasn't about to take whatever he cared to dish out now that she was an adult and had been through the hell of rehab.

The image made her open her eyes with a jolt of realization. She quickly amended the thought. Okay, so the rehab center had been sort of spalike, really. Even though at the time it had seemed so difficult. But she'd simply lain back and gotten through it.

Now she knew about hell only too well. The last couple of days, she truly had been there in horrible, living color. And lying back had not been possible.

Still, she had found something important in this disaster. Baby Tara, who was left in that hell. Bailey was determined to do whatever it took to get her out of there.

Including letting Hunter Long have his way. Temporarily. But when this was over and they were all safe, he would be sorry he'd ever treated her like this. She would find a way to make him see she deserved better.

"Jeez, that's cold," she gasped.

"Shush," he admonished as he scooped another handful of water over her feet. "This will help loosen the nylons. They have to come off so I can treat your blisters."

Bailey began to shake. "I...I can take them off." She stuttered through the shivers. "Or we can cut them away. They're snagged to bits anyhow."

She shook so badly that Hunter felt sure she would never be able to pull the hose off her own feet. Her weakened condition was worrisome.

Maybe it had been a mistake to even suggest taking her along. But there was nothing to do now except treat the wounds the best he could so they could be on their way.

"Lean back," he grumbled. "The material's attached to the dried blood on your skin. Plus, the nylon itself is too useful to waste. I'll get them off you."

Bailey crossed her arms over her waist and leaned against a flat rock. But her lips were a tight, straight line of frozen disapproval.

Too bad for her. He couldn't stop the smile from spreading over his face, which only succeeded in making her narrow her eyes at him.

Without thinking things all the way through, Hunter reached both hands up under what was left of her skirt. His fingers came in contact with the inside of her thigh, directly above her right knee. He stopped, frozen himself at the sudden reality of what he was touching.

Ah, hell.

This was going to take more willpower than he figured he had. Sighing deeply, he clenched his teeth and steeled his resolve. He was a good enough man to get through this without accosting her.

He wasn't anything like his dad.

A horrid image from long-ago, of his father abusing his mother, cooled Hunter's lustful thoughts in a New York minute. He was definitely a better man than *that*.

As gently as he dared, he let his fingers crawl up the silken skin of Bailey's thigh. Until his fingertips touched a wide band of elastic near her hip.

Despite the cool temperatures, sweat was rolling down his temples. But he managed to squeeze his big fingers under the elastic and begin lowering the nylon.

Wishing she were a perfect stranger, and that he had never before felt—or tasted—the tender skin beneath his knuckles, Hunter pulled the stocking past her knee and down to her ankle. As he reached the worst of the blisters on her heel, the hose came to a halt.

The flimsy material had glued itself to the skin with Bailey's dried blood. If he kept going he would reopen her wounds. Open, bleeding sores were dangerous in the remote desert.

This was going to take more than simple willpower—

for both of them. He stopped tugging and reached for the medicine bag at his waist.

"What's wrong?" she asked.

"Did you know I became a full-fledged *hataalii* since we last saw each other?" he asked, deflecting her question as he reached for his pack and the white headband he wore for ceremonies.

"No. I knew you had taken some classes to become a medicine man with one of your uncles, back in high school after your dad died, but I didn't realize you had finished the course."

"I'm still learning," he said as he fitted the sash around his forehead. "It's a lifelong vocation. But I have mastered a couple of things, and I know something about traditional cures. Your mind and body are not in harmony. That way leads to sickness. I will temporarily—"

"Not in harmony? I was kidnapped and abused. Whatever would make you think my harmony might be screwed up?" She was being sarcastic, but he knew she was frightened and hurt.

"Bailey," he murmured as gently as possible. "For years you have been ignoring your grandmother's Navajo teachings. Somewhere deep inside, you feel guilty about it. Your out-of-balance condition contributed to your problems with addiction. You've angered the *yei* and things will continue to go wrong until you eventually make that right.

"I'm afraid we don't have time for offerings or for full ceremonial sings," he continued when she only stared at him. "Once both you and the baby are safe, one of the other medicine men can work with you on regaining harmony. In the meantime, I'm going to do a pollen blessing over you and then apply a healing medicine to your wounds. Okay?"

"Uh, whatever. I guess."

Bailey's mind was swirling. Hunter suddenly seemed so different from the charming rogue she remembered from her childhood.

"Good." He took a piece of stone from his pouch. "Hold this sliver of turquoise in your hand and concentrate on its warmth."

"Sure."

Hunter closed his eyes and began to chant. It was a song she remembered, one that praised the four sacred mountains. As his voice grew stronger, the words and melody became so vibrant that the air fairly shimmered around her.

Spellbound, she was mesmerized by every word. Each syllable seemed to lighten her spirit. How could this man, who seemed so ethereal, be the same earthy, lusty Hunter Long she thought she'd known so well?

At last the song was over and he reached inside his bag for a handful of what looked like pollen. He touched the yellow granules to the tip of his tongue, then to the top of his head. Finally, he threw the rest of the pollen in the air above them both.

As pollen slowly rained down all over her, she felt different. Almost light-headed and giddy. Bailey blinked back tears. Her body aches had nearly disappeared.

"What just happened? Magic? Who have you become, Hunter?"

He opened his eyes and grinned that same old teenage-boy smile. "In order to heal the body, traditional Navajo healers believe it's important to heal the spirit first."

Coming up on his toes to crouch next to her, Hunter took her hand. "I have a salve I will use on your feet now, and then I want to work on your shoes. Still with me, beauty?"

She nodded, too confused to speak.

"Good." He reached into his backpack and withdrew a small, black plastic vial. "Mostly this balm consists of bracken fern and yarrow. But my cousin Ben's wife made it up for me and she added a touch of antibiotic, to be on the safe side."

Rubbing the salve over her feet, Hunter quietly hummed as he worked. Bailey had no idea who his cousin or his cousin's wife might be, but at this point she had placed her fate into all of their hands.

And Hunter's hands were certainly tender as he soothed and rubbed her toes and ankles. Before she knew it, the nylons were off and her feet felt better than ever before. It was incredible.

"I'm going to pop the heels off your shoes," he told her. He picked the left one up and gave it a twist. "If I'm lucky…"

The narrow heel snapped off neatly in his hand. "How about that? Good workmanship. I'll be able to fit a piece of tanned leather to the bottom with no trouble. That should help you get traction on the rocks."

Bailey watched in amazement as he pulled a thin piece of hide from his pack and set to work. The shoes would look more like moccasins by the time he was finished. But she still worried about having to put her feet back inside the tight leather.

"One more thing," Hunter said as he inspected his work-manship. "I spotted a small bush with powerful leaves over by those rocks. Hold on a second."

Fascinated, she watched him break off a handful and crush them in his palm. "These leaves are called 'pie-plant medicine' by the children."

He sifted them from his palm into her shoes. "Crushed,

they're soothing to the skin. Like baby powder. See how it feels now."

"O-kay. If you say so." She slipped her foot into the shoe he held out, thinking of Cinderella. "It feels…great. Perfect. That's amazing."

"Good." He did the same to the other, then reached out a hand to help her stand. "Up you go, then. It's daybreak. Time to be on our way."

She stood up, glanced around and realized gray shadows had begun to replace the darkness. Hunter bent to fill his canteen in the spring while she stretched out the kinks in her legs.

They were in an arid valley, surrounded by cottonwoods, with the sandstone cliffs beyond them. It would be beautiful if her memories of the creepy kidnappers weren't so strong.

But she didn't have the time or energy to linger and appreciate the view. Not when Tara needed them.

And not while her feelings about Hunter had suddenly become so conflicted. Lord, what would her shrink back at rehab have to say about all this?

A couple of hours later, Bailey was more worried about the sunburned condition of her nose than about what her shrink would say. But her feet didn't hurt, not a bit.

She guessed her body must be running on adrenaline, because she wasn't tired, either. Hunter was making it easy for her. He moved like his name implied, a hunter stalking his prey in ever tightening circles. But he always made sure Bailey stayed within sight.

And what a sight that was. Whew. His chest had filled out since their college days. He had stormy eyes. And, oh, man. Those long, dark eyelashes and that chestnut hair, tied back from his face with a leather thong, were breathtaking. It wasn't fair. How dare he look even better at thirty than he had at twenty-two?

For the sixth time since they'd begun, Hunter raised his hand and silently brought them to a stop. This time their resting place was under a scrawny tree. But it provided a little shade and the cool shadows felt good on her face.

"Drink another few sips of water while I scout ahead for a minute." Hunter put the canteen to his lips for a second and then handed it over. "Remember, not too much all at once. We have to make this last."

She did as he said and then sat down on a flat piece of limestone to wait. When he came back, Bailey was gingerly peeling the first layer of skin off her nose.

"Stop picking at that. You'll only make it worse. You need some salve," he said as he flung his pack to the ground. "Maybe we should have an MRE now, too. We're going to be climbing in a few minutes and we won't be able to stop for a while."

"Are they very far ahead? They can't climb very fast with the baby, can they?"

"They're not far." He shook his head and dabbed salve on her nose. "You need a hat."

"I didn't think Navajos were supposed to have the kind of skin that would burn," she complained.

"You're only half Navajo. But once we get that first layer of bilagaana off you, the good Navajo skin underneath will protect you."

She looked up at him. His face was a mask, sober and focused, but his eyes…those startling gray eyes were full of laughter.

"That's a joke, right?"

"Perhaps." He handed her an MRE. "The kidnappers are following an old sheep trail. It leads along the base of the Rabbit Ears Mesa. If we go up and over the notch, we can catch them before they reach the northern edge."

"Up and over?" She raised her chin and looked toward the tall, rocky peak behind her. "I don't know...."

He took her shoulder with a tender grip and studied her face. "I can help you. But you have to be sure you truly want to make it. Otherwise, you must stay here and I'll come back for you. But it might be late tomorrow before I can return with the baby."

She shook her head. "Don't leave me. I can make it."

"Eat, then. We'll go in a few minutes."

Hunter felt they were making good time as they climbed among the familiar red sandstone escarpments. He'd traveled both routes as a boy and knew the sheep path was more level, but it took twice as long to go that way.

He had tied Bailey's thigh-high nylons together and then to a length of rope he always carried. One end was around his waist and the other around hers in case she slipped. But she seemed steady enough so far.

She was keeping up quite well. He didn't want to think too long on how he felt about that, though. In fact, he'd rather not dwell on Bailey Howard at all right now.

They'd already passed the great outcropping of black shale. He knew the sight of the vast desert floor and the distant blue of Ute Mountain, over the Colorado state line to the east, would greet them around the next overhang.

Trying to concentrate on the possibilities of where the two kidnappers were headed was better than giving his emotions free rein. Worry and desire were the sworn enemies of a Navajo's innate sense of order.

He was fighting both at the moment. Silently, he reminded himself of a few of the ancient, sacred legends. He hoped the complicated and intense stories would free him of distractions. A Navajo made adjustments, found ways of remaining in harmony with the universe.

Hunter refused to let anger over the baby's treatment and the potentially fatal side effects of the sedation they were forcing on her work its furious panic into his mind. The familiar feel of Bailey's legs as he had rubbed salve into her skin was yet one more thought he sought to avoid.

Those distractions could get him killed.

In the distance, he heard the shrill call of a raptor flying high overhead. A stunted juniper jutted out of the rock just above him. They had arrived at the peak.

Holding up his hand to silently announce that they were stopping, he began to undo the rope from around his waist. Bailey took a few more steps upward and reached the ledge where he was standing.

"Why are we stopping?" she whispered.

He handed her the canteen. "We're at a point where we'll be able to see them below us. I'm going on up there—" he pointed straight up the side of the granite "—to do a little recon. You rest. I'll only be a few minutes."

She nodded. But as he removed the end of the rope from her waist, she grabbed his wrist with a deathly grip.

"Don't leave me here."

The slight tremor in her voice and the haunted look in her eyes did something to him. Something he couldn't name and refused to think about.

Pulling off his backpack, he handed it to her. "This is

our lifeline. Everything we need to stay alive out here. Hold on to it for me. I'll be back down as soon as I catch sight of the kidnappers."

Bailey hugged the twenty-five pound pack to her chest and stepped back into the shade of the overhang. "Hurry."

Scrambling up to the flat-topped pinnacle, Hunter eased down on his haunches and looked through the binoculars. It had been so long that he had almost forgotten the stark beauty of the landscape.

Spread out below him was every imaginable color of pink and red, where sandstone met limestone. In the distance, past the hard-packed sand, broken shale and gaudy marble veins in the limestone, stood a cinder block cabin he had nearly forgotten. Christian missionaries had built it forty years ago in the midst of the salt pines and sagebrush that sprang up around an artesian well.

Only a long-unused but still visible wagon track led up to it. He didn't see any vehicles parked nearby, not even the horse-drawn variety. The place had stood vacant for twenty years, but right then a curl of smoke lifted from the pipe in the roof.

The smell of the burning sheep dung reached his nostrils and he tested the wind. Hunter did not want his scent to carry on the downdrafts. He had not forgotten about the dog. But the wind was blowing in his favor.

Using the glasses, he checked the grasses and shallow arroyos surrounding the cabin. About fifty feet away was a newly dug trench and a large, circular flat spot maybe two hundred feet across the desert floor.

There was no movement. Hunter knew any noise would announce his presence throughout the landscape. So he slowed his breathing as he sat back and waited.

* * *

Bailey had listed the Narcotics Anonymous Twelve Steps in her head at least a hundred times before she finally heard a noise from above her. Funny, she really hadn't tried to memorize those steps while at rehab. It was interesting what kinds of things stuck in one's mind and came to the front at the weirdest times.

She tilted her head out from under the ledge and watched Hunter climb down beside her. "Did you see them?"

He nodded. "They met an old woman, Navajo grandmother type, who was waiting for them at a cabin near the well. She took the baby and gave them a piece of her mind."

Hunter chuckled as Bailey handed him the canteen. "The old lady didn't waste a moment outside by the well before she had the child cleaned up, redressed and fed. The kid was awake and playing with the woman by the time I saw them all go into the cabin."

"What are we going to do now?"

"The old grandmother said something about three days before the map would change hands. I'm guessing they intend to stay there, waiting for the ransom."

"A map? That seems odd. What do you suppose it means?"

Hunter shrugged. "Maybe it's a map meant for the baby's grandfather, so he'll be able to find her? But I have no intention of leaving that baby girl with those goons for another twenty-four hours, let alone three more days."

"What can we do?"

"We're going to wait until dusk, when the shadows will provide better cover. Then I'm going to sneak up to the cabin and take the child."

"It sounds dangerous."

He studied her for a moment. "Maybe you can provide the distraction we need to get Tara away safely."

"Me? Uh…" Bailey fought between her desire to get to Tara and her desire to save herself.

But she had come this far. She simply couldn't turn away now. The guilt trip would send her right back into the clutches of addiction.

"Okay. I guess I could do something like that. What'll we do in the meantime?"

"It's going to be over a hundred degrees on the floor of the desert near that cabin once the sun is high in the sky. Anyone with any sense stays in the shade and naps. I figure you have at least that much of a brain," he added with a wry grin.

Bailey fisted her hands on her hips. "Cute. Thanks. But where will we wait?" She threw a glance up the sheer rock wall he'd climbed down. "Not up there."

"No. But I do want to keep an eye on that cabin. I spotted a shallow cave in a cliff overlooking the valley. I'd almost forgotten about it. Coyotes use it as a den in winter, but…"

"Wild animals?" She shivered and shook her head. "Think of somewhere else."

He bent to shrug into the pack, then took her elbow. "Come on, Miss Howard. It's late summer, not winter. And besides, you're with me. I'm not about to let anything happen to me."

Chapter 5

"Now we have to go back up?" Bailey was winded from climbing along a path that had seemed easy and flat before. But it'd become so much hotter now that the sun was high.

Hunter turned, checked her out from head to toe with one quick glance and grunted. "You can't stay here. It's too exposed."

Damn frustrating man. "I can try climbing, I guess."

"No." He narrowed those beautiful gunmetal eyes at her. "Can you relax your muscles?"

"Relaxing sounds easy enough. Why?"

He didn't bother to answer, just grasped her around the waist and scooped her up bodily. Bailey found herself sharing his broad shoulder with half the backpack and staring down at his backside. A nice firm backside it was, too.

"Keep those muscles loose," he advised as he took the first step up a shale path. "And regulate your breathing."

The man was climbing almost vertically up the side of a cliff, with her weight added to the heavy pack. Bailey swallowed and closed her eyes. No way in the world could she manage to relax and watch the bottom drop out from under them at the same time.

She was beginning to understand now why her father had wanted Hunter to come for her. She'd had no idea how powerful and primitive he could be. At times he seemed more bloodhound than human. And now the guy she thought she'd known had suddenly become a superhuman comic book hero who could scale sheer walls.

It felt like hours since they'd started the climb. But just as nausea began clogging her throat, Hunter bent through a narrow opening and moved into a dark, much cooler place. Then he relaxed his shoulder and let her body slide down his.

Clinging to him for support, Bailey tried to steady herself, but her knees were wobbly.

Holding on to her with one strong arm, Hunter lowered the pack to the ground with the other. He was something else, this charming summer fling from her past.

Right then, the smell of the place hit her smack in the nostrils. Gamey. Musky. Wild.

She and Hunter weren't smelling all that wonderful themselves, what with the sweat and dirt and two days without brushing their teeth. But this new scent was a wild animal smell, and it reminded her of the coyotes.

Something rustled in the dark, and she jumped. The light was low in the cave and she shifted around, squinting into every dark corner.

"It's only insects and maybe a rabbit, beauty," Hunter crooned to soothe her. "Nothing will harm you. I'm right here."

His voice was so smooth and warm. His embrace so tight and safe. When he looked down into her face, smokey fire danced in his eyes.

Gratitude, appreciation, fear and exhaustion rushed over her in equal parts. Something…something perilous but hugely important was about to happen. She could feel it in every vein.

Bailey drew a breath and waited.

"You need to sit down a second," Hunter mumbled, and helped her to the ground. He tried to back away from the temptation. She was wounded and afraid, in no condition to do anything about the sizzle of heat between them.

He was a better man.

A memory of her as a college girl came out to devil him. The day on a cliff, when the breeze had tousled her thick, dark hair and her devastating, exotic eyes had glittered with potent feminine heat. He'd been blindsided by his emotions. Their tender friendship had suddenly changed into intoxicating but forbidden desire.

But even then he'd wanted more from her. Something he couldn't name and never got the chance to figure out. She was loving, gentle, rich and spoiled. A true paradox.

If he had let it, the hurt when she'd walked away without giving them a chance could've thrown him out of balance for good. He was too much Navajo for that, though.

"I'm going to find out how well we can see the cabin from here," he rasped past a suddenly dry throat. "We need to know how much they can see of us, too. I think we're pretty well hidden behind that shelf of rocks between us and the ledge, but I need to check it out.

"Have a drink of water while I'm gone." He handed her the canteen and turned. "I'll be right—"

"Don't leave me." She grabbed his leg and clutched at his knee. "Take me with you, or stay. But don't walk away."

The fear and anguish in her voice drove him to change direction and kneel beside her. "Easy, beauty. Everything's cool."

"Why do you keep calling me that? Beauty. What the heck does that mean?"

He heard the shrill tone, saw that her shoulders were beginning to shake. Reality was sinking in and she looked as if she was on the verge of shock.

Putting his arm around her shoulders to steady her, he lowered his voice. "I thought the nickname would be clear enough. You're the most beautiful woman I know.

"Besides," he continued rationally, "Traditional Navajos do not use proper names, remember? We're taught it's rude to use names. Doing so takes away the other person's power. As children we find nicknames for each other and use those instead. I chose 'beauty' because that's the way I've always thought of you."

Instead of smiling or at least saying thank-you, Bailey reared back and grimaced. "Damn you. There you go again. You're always so freaking charming and nice. Stop doing that. It's only a big lie, anyway. I look… I look…"

By now tears were streaming down her face and her chin trembled. Hunter knew it meant her body was finally reacting to the ordeal.

Tightening his grip on her shoulders, he slowly stroked her cheek, pushing back the tears. "You look more alive and sexy now than you ever have before," he whispered.

When she only groaned and squeezed her eyes closed, he briskly rubbed her arms to get the circulation going. "Listen to your heart beating." He could hear hers loud and clear from five inches away. "You're alive, and you're going to stay that way."

Bailey wasn't so sure. She couldn't hear anything, could barely feel anything. As warm as it had been a minute ago, she was freezing now. Her whole body began to shake.

"Why am I so cold?"

"Shock." He reached into his pack, took out a small folded package and opened it up to reveal a full-size jacket made from some fantastic new material. "Here, put this around you and stay close. Let my body heat warm you."

She gladly snuggled into his side while he wrapped the jacket tightly around her and held it closed. "I can't be in shock," she cried. "It's too late…or too soon. We haven't gotten Tara out yet."

"Shush. Rest. Give your body a chance to catch up. We'll get the baby tonight. Those goons do not stand a chance when you and I start working together."

Bailey shut her eyes and hung on to him. She still couldn't hear her own heart, but she heard his, beating strong and sure and secure.

She found herself nuzzling Hunter's neck. No huge surprise, but it suddenly wasn't safety she wanted from her former lover.

His hand stroked her back, but each slow movement stirred rather than soothed. Wanting to feel his palm on her bare skin, she tried to sneak out from under the jacket. Casually, she shrugged it off one shoulder and then flattened her breasts to his chest as if the sudden cool air on her naked arm had been a big shock.

The movement made a difference in Hunter's attitude right away. He tightened his grip and dragged her into his lap. In this position, his warm breath blew against her neck.

His nearness electrified her and sent shock waves of sensation to hidden regions.

Her every sense went on high alert. He smelled musky, manly, sexy as hell. His breathing became ragged, ripping into her core with each muffled pant. The hair on her skin crackled, and she was dying to feel his hands on all her sensitive places.

Raging memories of what they'd done in the past pushed her over the edge of reason. She twisted her body and threw her arms around his neck, pulling his head down for a kiss.

Their lips met as she dragged him closer with desperate need. Her heart jumped and stuttered as she put her whole being into the kiss, clinging to him as if this was her last chance to touch and be touched by a man.

Maybe it was.

Frustrated, Hunter broke off the kiss too soon, leaned his head back and stared at her. "Don't do this, Bailey. The heat is only aftershocks of adrenaline running through your system. It isn't real. You'd hate yourself later for giving in to it. Worse yet, you'd hate me."

"Never. You said you could never hate me. Well, I could never hate you, either."

Caught between paradise and hell, he hesitated. How could he have forgotten the pull of her kiss? Or the delicious sensation of having her breasts pressed against his chest?

The answer was simple. He hadn't forgotten at all, but had simply pushed the memory into a distant recess of his mind in order to save his sanity and maintain harmony in his life.

He wasn't about to go through that again. Not even for the promise of what he held in his hands.

"Easy does it," he said, more to himself than to her. "You need to rest and heal. Let me go outside for a minute and scout around. Here…"

He backed away and put the pack down in his place. "Use this for a pillow and sleep. Just for a little while. Okay?"

Tears welled in those golden-colored eyes, but she said nothing. It was hard not to take her in his arms and soothe her. Harder yet to turn away from the heat and the memories.

But he managed. He walked out into the sunshine, chanting silently a traditional prayer for balance and harmony.

> The universe is walking with me
> In beauty it walks before me
> In beauty it walks behind me
> In beauty it walks below me
> In beauty it walks above me
> Beauty is on every side
> As I walk, I walk with beauty

Bailey raised her head. She could've sworn she smelled smoke. How long had she been out? It might've been only a minute. She could still feel the buzz of tension running through her veins from needing Hunter.

She blinked, and he was there, bending over her.

"Ah, you're awake. Good. Are you hungry?"

"Hungry?" It took a second for the word to make sense. "Starved." She sat up and looked around. "You built a fire?" Stupid question. The truth was easy to see from a shallow pit glowing with red-orange light.

"It's dusk," he answered patiently. "The smoke won't be seen and that shelf of granite in front of the cave entrance will hide the light from the fire. I checked."

"Dusk," she gasped, and reached out for him. "The baby. We have to go get her."

"Soon." Hunter took her hand. "I want you to put hot

food in your stomach first. And I have something I want to tell you before we prepare a rescue."

She sniffed and was assaulted by the smell of meat. "What are you cooking?"

She'd spent a full year as a designer vegetarian once, back when that was considered hot. But she had never gotten over how her mouth watered when the smell of cooking meat permeated the air. It was divine.

He stood, grinning and holding out a hand to help her up. "Rabbit stew. Not exactly epicurean fare, but nutritious. And pretty good, if I do say so myself."

She let him lead her closer to the fire pit. It was warmer here, nice…almost cozy. She rubbed her arms.

"The temperatures are starting to drop now that the sun's gone down. Here, put on the jacket, then sit down. You can wash your hands before you eat."

Nodding, she stuck out each arm and let him fit the jacket around her. "Do you have hot water and soap, too?"

Hunter laughed. "It's not magic, I swear. The nearest spring is down in the desert beside the cabin. It would've been great to get enough water for a bath, but too dangerous to spend much time so close. How about you use this bottle of hand sanitizer instead?" He grinned and held out a squeeze bottle that looked exactly like one she carried in her own purse while traveling.

"I can't believe you have anything so…so…"

"Civilized?" he supplied.

She ignored the comment and reveled in using the fresh-smelling sanitizer on her hands and face. She felt almost human again.

He dished up some stew, and she marveled at how clever he'd been about pots and utensils. Hollow rocks and smooth pieces of wood, roughly carved into plates. He handed her a metal expandable spoon and dug into the pot himself, using a wide, flat knife as a utensil.

"You've been busy this afternoon," she joked after swallowing a couple of delicious bites. "This is great. I don't recognize any of the flavors, but it's all good."

"It's one of my aunt's recipes for on the trail. She uses mutton in place of rabbit, but the rest of the ingredients are from things found near here. Glad you like it."

A few swallows later Hunter set down the pot and sat back on his haunches. "Bailey," he began in a serious tone. "There has been no sign of movement coming from the cabin. No lights or fires now that it's dusk. No smoke or sounds all afternoon. It concerns me."

She dropped her spoon. "What about Tara? What do you think has happened?"

"They have not left that cabin in any of the usual ways," he told her. "I placed a thread of pine bark in the path in front of the door right after you fell asleep this morning. It's still there. And most of the windows are nailed shut."

Hunter grimaced and then studied her face in the firelight. "I'm going to tell you a story. It'll sound fantastic and impossible, but I promise you that it's true. Will you trust me not to lie to you?"

"Why wouldn't I?" She spat out the words without thinking.

He scowled and she forced herself to slow down. "I trust you with my life, Hunter. If you say the moon is blue cheese, I will believe it."

Giving a small nod, he began. "Well, keep an open

mind. Do you remember your grandmother ever telling you the Skinwalkers' legend when you were small?"

"The witches? Sure. It was thrilling. Scary. All hush-hush kid stuff. Why?"

"Let me tell you the legend again. My way this time."

She nodded and waited, ready to believe almost anything. If perfectly civilized people could be kidnapped and dragged through the remote wilderness—and then saved by an old boyfriend who turned out to be superhuman, in a sexy survivalist's disguise—then anything was possible.

"According to Dine legend, Sun married Turquoise Woman and had two sons, Monster Slayer and his twin, Child of Water. The two young men became great warriors and set out to rid the world of monsters. But they deliberately left four monsters alive—Cold, Hunger, Poverty and Death. Their reasons for doing so became the stories for another legend.

"This legend goes on to say one monster escaped without their knowledge," Hunter continued. "That monster was known as Greed, and he hid from them in a deep cave under a body of water. Sometime later, Diving Heron plunged into the water and brought back Greed's knowledge and secrets, contained in sacred parchments. Diving Heron turned the secrets over to a medicine man, who quickly learned to control them. He was able to change himself into any animal with extraordinary powers, and he did so to gain power and wealth. This medicine man became the first evil one. A Skinwalker."

Bailey felt shivers run down her spine. Hunter seemed so serious as he calmly discussed an old legend she'd always believed was simply a Navajo grandmother's tale. It was chilling.

"The first Skinwalker recruited others to his side, but he had one secret he refused to share with anyone. That secret was longevity—the power to live forever. With that power, he lived for a thousand years. When he finally sought the relief of death, the evil one told Diving Heron to replace the parchments holding those secrets back in the cave under the water so no one would ever find them."

Hunter stopped talking and took a sip from the canteen. Then he stayed quiet and watched her. It felt like that last moment before an envelope was slit open, revealing bad news. He must be waiting for some sign to continue, she guessed.

"Go ahead," she told him. "I don't understand what this has to do with us, but I'm listening."

"There have been many Skinwalkers throughout the ages. Most of them have taken the form of the head witch known as the Navajo Wolf, but throughout the years their legions have taken other animal forms, as well. Today…"

Hunter stopped, took a breath and seemed to make up his mind about something. "A few years ago, a mysterious man appeared in Dinetah. Evil and powerful, this man apparently found some of the old scared parchments. He's gathered an army of greedy men who've learned to turn themselves into superpowerful animals. This army has been causing the Dine huge problems, so—"

"What? Wait a minute. You're serious, aren't you? You really believe this stuff."

"Bailey," he said with a shake of his head. "You said you trusted me to tell the truth. Listen to me. I have joined a secret group of Dine medicine men sworn to find and kill off the evil ones. We call ourselves the Brotherhood."

She caught herself shaking her head, denying his words without saying so.

"I've seen them," Hunter insisted softly. "I've done battle with creatures you would not believe. We lost a good friend in one skirmish, but we have taken out a number of them, as well. You would have to see it to…"

He stopped talking and stared over the fire at her. "You *have* seen it, haven't you? You know what I say is true because you've seen one with your own eyes."

"No," she hedged. "It was a bad dream. A nightmare caused by exhaustion."

"Where? When did you see it?"

"On the shuttle bus," she told him with a shaky breath. "Right before the crash. Two eyes appeared at the window—yellow, scary, impossible eyes. And then there was this strange dog growling. I thought I was dreaming."

Hunter stood and paced toward the narrow cave opening. "This *is* Skinwalker doing, then. I was afraid of that." He came back and squatted beside her. "We might not be able to get the baby back tonight. They may have spirited her away somehow. But we will find her. We will rescue her. I swear it.

"We'll go down now and check the cabin. But you must not be disappointed when we find they are gone."

She reached out and gripped his arm. "You promised we would save Tara. I can't really believe all this stuff. But if it's true, what'll we do?"

He pried her hand from his arm and held it in his warm palm. "We'll gather evidence. And we'll wait for help. I think I'll be able to send the Brotherhood a message at first light. By late tomorrow we'll have assistance."

Bailey couldn't stop the tears that threatened. The situation was ridiculous. How could you battle witches? And how could everything that had seemed so dark and dangerous suddenly become so much worse?

Throwing herself into Hunter's arms, she collapsed against him and sobbed.

A sliver of moon cast a glow around the peaks of a phantom thundercloud. Hunter moved like a cat, quiet and unseen in the near darkness. Bailey felt more like an elephant, stomping along in the rear and checking behind her at every step.

Skinwalkers came out at night. All Navajos knew that. So what was she doing out here on the desert floor, so exposed in the pitch-dark?

Hunter had given her the plan to create a diversion. She hoped to have enough courage to follow through. If she could only get a shot of brandy, or maybe a half-dozen cosmopolitans, to help her stay strong, things would look much better. Gritting her teeth, she tried to keep up.

A few moments later he stopped, turned, grabbed her up in a tight embrace. "It's time," he whispered directly in her ear.

Through both their jackets, she could feel him breathing. His body fairly shimmered with tension.

"Wait for the signal. Light the fire, then move to your left as fast as you can. Got it?"

She nodded, and he slipped away.

Don't be surprised by the noise, he'd told her. Stay calm. Calm? No way. Her heart was pounding so loudly in her chest she was positive no other sound diversion should be necessary.

Going over and over his instructions in her head, Bailey

remembered to count to twenty slowly. But as she got to nineteen, the whole world exploded in a noisy clamor. Horrible, loud screeches seemed to be surrounding her, coming from exactly where she stood.

That must be Hunter's signal. He'd told her not to be surprised. But…hell.

With hands shaking and ears ringing, Bailey lit the match to set fire to the creosote branch she carried. Another explosion, this time of flame and heat. She had no trouble remembering to drop the branch, then turn and run.

She didn't fall, thank heaven. Nor did she stop, until the base of the cliff loomed a few feet ahead.

Finally, out of breath and with her knees giving way, she collapsed behind a rock and squeezed her eyes shut. Hugging herself to keep her heart from jumping right out of her chest, Bailey waited.

Hunter was unnerved, which seldom happened anymore. What he'd found was not totally beyond possibility. Still, the technology of it had surprised him.

He crept over the desert floor until he reached the base of the cliff, wishing he had better news for Bailey.

Where had she gone, anyway? He stopped, listened, then actually heard her breathing. It automatically brought a smile to his face. She'd done exactly what he'd told her to do, even though he knew she'd been scared beyond reason.

Not counting on her to see it through, he'd had a secondary plan. But she'd done her job and then taken herself out of the way so he needn't worry about her. She had turned into one tough little princess.

He moved closer and called out in a whisper, "Bailey, it's me. Stay where you are. I'm on my way."

When he found her crouched behind a boulder, he knelt and pulled her close. "I'm proud of you. We made a good team."

"What was that god-awful noise?" she croaked. "How'd you do that?"

"I threw my voice. Made it sound like cats fighting. The hunters and warriors of old knew how to do such things. It's a skill that can come in handy."

"Well…yeah, I guess so. What about Tara?" Bailey's voice cracked, and he wished there was something good to tell her.

"Gone. The cabin was empty, as I feared."

"But how? Where'd they go?"

"There's a massive tunnel hidden under the floorboards. I climbed down and followed it as far as I dared. That must be how they all got away."

"Let's go back," she cried. "We'll go into the tunnel and find where they took Tara."

He shook his head and grimaced. "Not a good idea, I'm afraid. These are Skinwalkers. They have superhuman hearing and sight. No matter how quiet we tried to be, they'd hear our footsteps echoing down the tunnel a mile away. And we'd be no help to Tara if they caught us down there."

"But…"

"The tunnel must lead somewhere," he told her. "I'm betting it goes to some kind of underground cave where the Skinwalkers can hide without fear of being discovered. There has to be another way in and out. We'll find it. But we need the Brotherhood's help."

"You said that last night. How are we going to call them?"

"At first light we can begin scouting for the other entrance. I'm sure the Bird People will have been notified to be on the watch for us by then. We'll send a message to the Brotherhood through them."

"The *Bird* People?"

"Never mind. You'll see tomorrow. But right now we need to get out of the open and stay hidden until dawn. We don't want to take any chances of being discovered."

"Where are we going?"

He glanced up the cliff and grinned. "Back home, Miss Howard. Back to your coyote den."

Chapter 6

Home? Not anywhere close. The place was dark and dank and just plain creepy.

But up they went. And this time she climbed under her own power. The sleep, the food and following through with their plan had all combined to make her feel stronger.

After squeezing through the cave opening, Hunter squatted to stoke the fire. "I brought piñon needles up here while you slept to use as a cushion," he told her. "Sit. The fire will warm things in a few minutes."

She plopped down on the comfortably soft needles and stared at him across the blue-and-orange flames. Who was this man, really? Her whole life had turned upside down, but nothing was as confusing as he was.

"What made you decide to join the Tribal Police?" she asked.

"You don't remember?" His voice was soft, tentative.

When she didn't answer, he turned away to grab more pieces of wood for the fire. "No, I don't suppose you do. We only spoke of futures once in the whole time we dated."

"I can't remember ever talking…at least about ambitions," she said with a half smile. "I only remember the heat, and all that urgency, whenever you got anywhere close."

Bailey knew that she'd been wrong. She hadn't taken his ideas or feelings seriously. But she had been young and definitely foolish. And so swept up with her newly discovered lust that she had barely thought of anything save for their next kiss, their next stolen moment alone.

Hunter grunted and looked up at her with a grin. "Yeah. You were hot. I remember that all too well."

From the tone of his voice, she didn't know whether that was a compliment or a criticism. Of all the nerve. As if she'd been the only one to rush into their affair. As if he had never charmed his way into her jeans.

Irritation swamped her, but she refused to knuckle under to it. He was her lifeline, her way around the Skinwalkers and Tara's only hope.

No, she needed him too much to start a fight. She decided to try again.

"Can you tell me now why you wanted to become a cop? I'll really listen this time."

"Don't know if you'll remember me telling you this, either," he began with an almost charming smirk, "but my father was a retired U.S. Marshal officer when he brought the family back to my mother's home in Dinetah. He'd been honored and cited for his work in the service as its number one disguise master."

"I do remember you telling me about how important the person is who makes the disguises for the people the

Marshal's service protects. I thought that job sounded so cool. He died, didn't he?"

"A couple of years before I met you." Hunter gave a sharp nod. "He was assassinated. Someone put a bullet into the back of his skull, ran his car off a cliff and then burned the evidence. No one has ever been charged for the crime."

"So you became a cop in his honor? Or to find his killer?"

"Neither, exactly. My brother, Kody, became an FBI agent in his memory, but I don't have those same feelings."

Hunter sat back, folded his long legs under him.

Bailey could hear the controlled anger lacing his words. It fascinated her. She decided to be nosy.

"You sound as though your father may have treated you and your brother differently."

"Yeah. Kody doesn't see it this way, but he was lucky. My parents sent him off to federal boarding schools at the time we moved back here to the Four Corners. I was the baby— in the Navajo tradition, my mother's family needed me in the summers. My father needed me the rest of the time."

Hunter watched her reactions carefully. He'd never said these things to anyone.

"What did your father do here in Dinetah?"

Anything except what was legal or moral, Hunter thought grudgingly to himself. He wasn't sure about being open with her.

But he wouldn't lie. Bailey was too important to lie to.

"Supposedly, my father had been hired to help the Tribal Police set up their brand-new, state-of-the-art communication and investigative outposts. He was only one-eighth Navajo, and hadn't been too interested in his heritage. So he dragged me along to the remote areas of Dinetah in order to translate and teach him how to get along with the traditionalists."

"You said 'supposedly.' What does that mean?"

"I believe my father was living a double life. Many times I saw him exchange money with some rather shady looking characters. I was even there one day when I think he killed someone."

"Killed? Really?"

Hunter nodded sharply, then looked away. "He'd sent me back to the car. And I thought…well, he'd done that kind of thing a few times. At the houses of women I had never seen before. Not relatives. Not even all of them Navajos."

"Oh. I'm so sorry—"

He waved his hand, cut off her words. "Skip the sentiment. It didn't matter in the end. But that one night I remember noises, like shots being fired. And he came flying back to the car, and we took off with tires squealing.

"He refused to talk about what had happened. A few days later I saw a newspaper headline that said a man and his wife had been killed by an intruder at that same address in Gallup."

"So you think he went there to rob them?"

"Not at all. I think the husband came in and caught my old man in bed with his wife. The guy probably shot the woman in anger, but then my father shot him. That's what makes the most sense."

"How old were you then?"

"Thirteen."

"So young to know such awful things."

There had been worse, he mused. Things he had seen right in his own home.

"Not all of us had two parents who were loving and protective," he said before he thought about it.

Bailey reared back as though he'd slapped her face. But

instead of saying anything, she wrapped her arms around herself and put her chin on her knees.

He would've said he was sorry, but what for? Pointing out that she had been lucky, but never appreciated it?

"So why a cop?" she finally asked.

"Justice," he said simply. "Someone needs to uphold the law and traditions. I want to be the one.

"That's partially why I joined the Brotherhood," he continued. "I like things when they are in harmony, the way they're supposed to be. I'm willing to work hard and take risks to set things on the right path."

Time to change the subject. He turned the conversation back to her. "So how'd you end up in rehab?"

She lifted her chin and stared him down. "I went when I was so sick there was no other choice."

"But why did you let yourself get to such a state?"

"All my parents ever expected from me was to find happiness," she began, her voice hoarse. "They gave me every advantage and loved me beyond measure. But I didn't…don't have the foggiest idea how to capture that elusive happiness. I've tried school, business, skiing, yacht racing, gambling, lots of other stuff. But none of it gave me a real reason to get up in the morning.

"I'd thought," she added slowly, "for a few moments back in college, that you were the answer to all my problems."

"Me?"

"I was really happy with you." She gave a self-depreciating chuckle. "I jumped out of bed every morning and couldn't wait until I got to see you again."

"Bailey…" His own voice deserted him.

"I know now that's unreasonable. That no other person can make you happy," she added. "But it really hurt when you didn't seem to feel the same way I did. Nothing had ever hurt me quite like that before. All my life, people always loved me. I didn't understand that not everyone automatically would."

He had hurt her? The idea was incongruous, so different from what he had always believed, that he couldn't get his mind around it.

Just like that, Hunter's entire world tilted somehow. Ease and loss of control both suddenly became unimportant.

"Did you ever find someone to love?" she asked before he got his bearings. "Are you married? Any kids?"

It grew much too warm in the cave. The fire leaped and crackled between them. Hunter shrugged out of his jacket, but felt as if he were burning alive. So he pulled his shirt over his head and kicked off his moccasins.

Naked from the waist up, he finally felt as if he wasn't suffocating, as if he wasn't about to swallow his own tongue. "There have been a few women in and out of my life since college," he managed to answer. "But I never married. No children. Don't think I'd be very good at being a dad."

Bailey swept her eyes up and down his torso. "It's hot in here all of a sudden, isn't it?" She took off the jacket and folded it. "I sure wish I could take a shower." She grimaced. "I feel gritty, grimy." Rubbing her legs with her hands, she seemed embarrassed and irritated at her filthy condition.

Hunter moved to her side, picked up sand and ashes and mixed them in his palms. "Maybe I've spent too much time alone in the wilderness," he said. "But a little earth and sweat only seem sensual. Our ancestors used a combination of warm ash and desert sand as soap. Here, let me show you how it works." He swiped the back of his hand across his own sweaty brow, wiping away wetness so he could see, and then picked up one of her feet. Flipping off her shoe, he briskly rubbed her long leg.

Her soft gasp when he touched the back of her knee finally slowed him down. He looked into her large, liquid eyes and his heart jerked. His blood began churning with primal, primitive lust. His skin felt as if it dripped with a savage longing so strong he had to clench his teeth to keep from acting on it immediately.

Excitement snapped in the air between them, but neither of them moved. Afraid of losing his head completely, Hunter tried to fight the overpowering hunger that threatened to consume every oxygen molecule in the cave.

"You have a streak of ash across your forehead," she said in a whisper, breaking the tension, yet somehow managing to stir it further. "Like an ancient warrior. It's…sexy."

Suddenly she was panting as though she'd been running a marathon. The expression she wore was raw, needy. Her gaze fixed on his mouth. Reaching toward the edge of the fire pit, she, too, picked up a handful of ash, but her eyes stayed trained on his face.

"You need a few more slashes of color. Here…" She gently swiped her thumbs across his cheekbones. "And here…" Her fingers drew a dark mark down the center of his chest to his waistband.

Her touch was both heady and intoxicating, and Hunter was doomed in that instant.

"And you, too…" He reached over and brushed aside the shredded rags that had been covering her breasts, leaving her exposed to both his gaze and his touch.

Picking up another fistful of warm ash, Hunter dribbled

it in the center of her breastbone. Then he circled her nipples with his thumbs, leaving black lines that resembled bull's-eyes. Her body became a tender target that beckoned his fingers to hit their satin mark.

Bailey reached out and fumbled with the zipper on his pants, silently calling to him with her eyes. Hunger ignited, deep and low, in some hidden, basic place.

Without a word he moved closer, slid his hand around to cup the back of her neck and allowed his mouth to crush hers in an incendiary kiss. It wasn't soft and tender—or even civilized.

He wanted to possess her. Beyond reason. With need both savage and feral. So, as never before, he took what his body demanded.

The punch of heat from Hunter's kiss made Bailey's heart jump. She plunged her tongue inside his waiting mouth, pressed her breasts against his chest and shoved at the dark suede pants encasing what she craved to touch.

Purring when she discovered he wasn't wearing underwear, Bailey all at once wanted everything. Her savage warrior had gone commando, and the knowledge made her blood sizzle and her brain fry.

She ran her hands over his shoulders, then down his biceps. His body was wider, tougher than she remembered. All those nights she'd ached for his touch, sighed for just one glimpse of that damn grin, and now he was here, tasting ripe and strong, like the earth itself. Her brain couldn't keep up, and she didn't care a bit.

Their bodies were slick with sweat, and all around them the air they breathed was heated and feverishly erotic. She freed and then caressed his arousal. Instinctively she fisted her hand around him and drew him upward.

Bailey didn't want slow and easy, nor tender and gentle, as their lovemaking had been in the past. Hunter's muscular and toned body staggered her senses. His masculine scent was addictive and heady.

She pulled out of his arms long enough to shove her panties down and kick them free. Hunter leaned back and watched her.

Straddling him where he sat, she ran her hands into his hair. He captured a nipple in his mouth, and some kind of ancient hunger moved through her, igniting a fierce female frenzy.

She lowered herself to where the tip of his body met the waiting warmth of her own. He stared up into her eyes with a look that was both crazily familiar and peppered with a stranger's need.

Hunter didn't hesitate. When he saw his feelings reflected in Bailey's eyes, he thrust forward to where he longed to be. She hooked her legs around his waist and gasped as he drove as far as he could go.

He took possession of her mouth and found her wild and edgy, grinding her hips restlessly into his groin. His fingers snagged in her hair; his lungs constricted. Her taste was potent and salty, carnal. He wanted to savor more, savor everything.

Their slick, slippery bodies began to move in rhythm, and soon the air sang with the rapid slide of flesh against flesh.

She bit his shoulder then threw back her head and arched her back, taut like a bow. A bundle of pure sensation ready to explode, she was every bit as rough as he felt. He placed his mouth on her neck and bit down, trying to hold her to him.

She screamed his name as her internal muscles finally convulsed around him. The blinding, searing joy stripped him of his last bit of sanity. She gave a keening cry of release and he damn near howled as his own body responded.

Still sobbing out his name, she clung to him. Caught in some twisted vortex of past and present, Hunter locked her in his embrace and let his own tears flow.

Hours later, Hunter lifted his head as he heard the desert winds pick up outside their cave. Bailey stirred in his arms.

Shaken to his foundations by what they had done, what he had done, he tried to find his center. Somehow, this hot woman's sensual draw had captured his spirit. He'd done as he had never intended. And he hated himself for the lapse of control.

Bailey sensed the change in the air and opened her eyes. Stretching along the length of him, she tried to think. She wanted to say something, to tell him how monumentally important what they'd done had been for her. But she was still lost in sensation.

"I…" She cleared her throat and tried again. "That was really something."

"Something?"

She didn't like his suddenly stern tone, and she nearly wept when he took her by the shoulders and rolled her aside.

The blast of cold that hit her was as much emotional as it was physical.

"For heaven's sake, can't we just say it was fun?" She forced herself to speak the words flippantly, with a roll of her eyes. "So much so, let's do it again. Right now."

But just then the wind shifted and an eerie howl blasted through their warm cave, scaring her spitless. Ohmigosh. She reached for Hunter, trying to climb right inside him.

He sat up and pulled her close. "Easy. That's probably

only a lonely coyote, or maybe a stray dog looking for the rest of its pack. Not to worry."

Unable to speak, she burrowed her nose in the crook of his neck and whimpered. Her body shuddered uncontrollably.

Hunter stroked her hair and murmured soothing words she didn't understand. When the shakes subsided, he pulled back and lifted her chin.

"None of this is a game," he told her softly. "The Skin-walkers are not just legends, they're all too real. I'm ashamed of myself for losing control with you—especially in the middle of danger. I took something that wasn't offered. I've never done anything so rash in my life."

Embarrassed, vulnerable and not sure what to say, Bailey decided to stick with being flip. "Well, you were sure good at it."

He moved away, zipped himself up and stoked the embers of the fire. "I…we…" He cleared his throat. "I didn't use protection. Didn't even consider it. I apologize. But I want you to know I'm healthy. The Brotherhood took vows of celibacy a couple of years ago and I have been true to that vow, until tonight."

"Celibacy? As in no sex? For two years?"

She could swear he was blushing. But maybe it was the glow of the firelight that gave his cheeks that rosy flush.

"Okay. That's cool, I guess." But something was bugging her. And of course, like an idiot, she let it all come popping out of her mouth. "Wait a minute. You talk like I either had nothing to do with what just happened…or maybe had everything to do with it. I was a willing participant. You didn't force me. Not even close."

"Bailey…" He reached out for her.

"No." She batted his hands away. "I wanted it to happen,

yes. I've dreamed about being with you again for years. But I didn't force you, either. And for your information," she declared, "I'm healthy, too. They checked us out at rehab. I'm a drug addict—but I didn't use needles and I'm not a sex addict."

Except when she was around him. But that didn't seem like the right thing to say at the moment.

He could barely look her in the eye. His body language said he regretted what they had done.

God, this was so frustrating and sad. Considering the danger they were in and how close they had to stay in order to remain alive, the two of them should be growing more intimate, learning each other's moves. Instead, she couldn't understand him at all.

Okay, he'd had a bad childhood and that sucked. But she'd heard much worse in group therapy. She couldn't relate to such things, but knew that talking about them with someone who cared was the only way to climb out of wallowing in pain.

Afraid she was falling in love again with a man who still could not, or would not, care about her, Bailey felt miserable all over. Her body and mind ached for him. But there was nothing she could say to change things, so she sat up and straightened what was left of her clothing.

Staying alive. Saving Tara. Bailey had to concentrate on the things potentially within her power.

Hunter saw annoyance spike in Bailey's eyes, but he was helpless to do anything about it. He'd let her tip him out of balance again. When they were safe, he would find a *hataalii* who knew the right sings to cure them both. But Hunter would be no help to her or the child unless he found harmony now.

The continued loss of his own control would make him useless. He closed his eyes and chanted a prayer of spirit harmony and promised himself it would not happen again.

"Are you hungry?" he asked her moments later, in as noncommittal a voice as possible. "Dawn is right around the corner. We'll be free to look for that other way into the Skinwalkers' hideout."

"I don't eat breakfast. But I'd give my right arm if you could conjure up a little coffee right now, medicine man."

He ignored her teasing jab, but couldn't help a small one of his own. "Isn't caffeine just another addiction, slick? Just another way of hiding from yourself?"

Her face paled and she jerked upright on shaky legs. "You're one to talk about hiding from how you feel. I've never seen anybody so…"

She paused and had the grace to look flustered. Waving her arms around the cave, she changed the topic. "I need to get out of this place. It's creepy, dark and claustrophobic. If the sun's coming up, let's go."

Hunter couldn't agree more. He needed the sunshine. Needed to be out in Dinetah where he belonged.

He nodded and threw sand on the fire. "Put your shoes on, Miss Howard. We have a long day ahead of us."

After taking a few moments outside for a dawn chant, Hunter led the way down the cliff. At the bottom, he glanced around and listened for any sounds that seemed out of place.

As he looked toward the canyon floor, the whole world suddenly turned vermillion. The dramatic beauty of dawn in his sandstone desert was breathtaking. The sky was luminescent, a shade of pure blue that shimmered with the sun's golden highlights. If he lived to a thousand, he would never get tired of this sight.

"Isn't it gorgeous?" Bailey's voice was filled with all the wonder that he felt.

He turned to her and for the second time in a minute lost his power of speech. She was magnificent, with the sun's rays making her skin glow and those same golden highlights shine in her eyes.

Wanting her, needing to possess her, Hunter stood speechless and immobile. He couldn't do this. Couldn't be with her. Yet he could not bear to walk away.

Fortunately, the shrill call of a hawk hunting for its morning meal brought him back to the present. Back to the war.

As a warrior must be willing to do, Hunter swallowed his needs. He vowed to stick with the real world and let go of all things that were…impossible.

Chapter 7

They had been walking through narrow rock canyons for so long that Bailey was becoming disoriented. Everything looked the same.

It had only been a couple of hours. Not even time enough for the sun to rise high in the sky. But that was part of the reason she felt so uncomfortable. There was no possible way to judge time or space.

From these confining canyons she could look up and see the sparkling cerulean sky beyond flashy red sandstone spires. Fabulous vistas, but they all looked exactly the same.

Turning one more corner, Hunter stopped her with a gentle hand as she followed him. "Look. Down there." He pointed and she swung around. "From here you can get a good view of the desert floor and the empty cabin."

She hadn't even realized they'd been climbing as they followed the rocky paths. But when Bailey focused, she got an excellent glimpse back to where they'd started. It seemed like a long way.

Hunter offered her the canteen. She hesitated. Not really thirsty, she would rather save the precious water.

"Take a sip," he urged. "You can easily dehydrate in the desert and never realize it. Sunstroke and heatstroke are usually not far behind, so drink."

He squatted on his heels as she leaned against a granite outcropping and took a few swallows. He raised the binoculars and studied the canyon floor below them.

"Ah. I remember now," he said from behind the glasses. "About six months ago the Tribal Police took reports from two different shepherd families in this area. They claimed to have seen a helicopter crash into the desert.

"When we checked, there were no missing helicopters reported. A flyover was done, but no wreckage was ever sighted."

"You're thinking that big cleared circle near the cabin is a heliport?"

"Yeah." He dropped the glasses and rubbed his eyes. "I imagine they used it to bring in the equipment necessary to dig the tunnel. The shepherds must've mistaken a controlled landing for a crash. That would certainly be easy to do in all these canyons."

"But where does the tunnel lead? Where could it go? And are you sure they didn't just swoop in and take Tara away in a helicopter?"

He lifted the binoculars again and studied the northern horizon. "We would've heard the 'copter land. We weren't that far away. Any noise travels in these canyons.

"Stay still a second, Bailey," he added suddenly. "Listen. What am I hearing?"

She lowered the canteen and tried to sort through the sounds around them. Normal calls from distant birds echoed in her ears. She closed her eyes and tried to block them all, along with the whooshing in her ears from her own breathing.

Concentrating hard, Bailey distinctly heard low murmurs. Under the white noise of the day there seemed to be a hum. And under that, farther away and weak, was another sound—both exciting and terrifying.

"I hear a baby crying," she squeaked. "I swear to God. It's Tara. It must be."

"Shush," Hunter whispered. "Your voice carries."

"Well, what do *you* hear?" She let the irritation lace her low whisper. The frustrating man had *asked* for her opinion.

He stood beside her so he could whisper in her ear. "I hear running water. It must be the San Juan to the north of us. Just over the horizon. I hadn't realized we were that close to the river. But I also hear a mechanical humming," he added. "Generators, most probably. Coming from underground. We must be standing right over the cavern they're using as a hideout."

"How do we get there? How will we find Tara?"

"Let me think a minute." He leaned against the outcropping and closed his eyes.

Bailey clamped her mouth shut and stared down at the desert floor. The winds were still strong and a crazy dust devil twirled across the cleared heliport area. From the other direction, a huge tumbleweed rolled right up to the cabin and stayed there, held in place by the wind.

Hunter turned to her again. "Have you ever gone down the San Juan River? Either on the rapids past Glen Canyon or the narrower, quieter stretches around Montezuma Creek?"

She shook her head. The East River and the Pacific at Malibu Beach were as close as she had ever gotten to large bodies of water in the past.

"It's beautiful and wild," he told her. "Russet sandstone buttes rise right up from the water's edge. Occasionally, a cavern or a cave indentation seems to magically appear in the cliffs beside the river. A couple of those caves are rumored to be several miles deep, with side chambers and tributaries that go off toward the desert and upward into the buttes."

"You think the river's edge will be the other way into the cavern?"

"Maybe. But if it is, we haven't got much of a chance of finding it. The entrance will only be accessible by water, and then only by those who know where it is. You can bet it will be guarded every minute."

Bailey swiped the back of her hand across her mouth, trying to get rid of the sweat on her upper lip. And at the same time trying to stem the scream of frustration that threatened to erupt. Damn it.

Hunter studied her a second. "Don't give up. I suspect that at least one of the tributaries runs past these cliffs. That has to be why we heard the baby's cry. The opening we seek may be small, maybe too narrow for us to fit through. But we should still look for it."

"Yes. I'm sure I wasn't dreaming a minute ago. I heard Tara. We have to keep looking."

He nodded. "We will. But there's a couple of other things we have to do first."

"Like what?"

Reaching into his shirt pocket, he pulled out another interesting vial, like the one that held the salve for her feet. "I'm becoming more and more concerned about that dog.

Where is it? Is it guarding the cliffs? Or the river entrance? I don't like not knowing."

Hunter gave her a sideways grin. "This isn't pleasant, but let me put some of this liquid on the back of your ankles. For protection."

"What is it?" She had visions of him telling her it was magic dust. Some of his cures and ideas were a little eccentric.

"Skunk musk. It will confuse the—"

"Skunk? No way in hell. Keep that stuff away from me."

"Bailey…"

"No. My feet have got calluses on top of calluses. My hair is a stringy disaster. My poor acrylic nails are cracked and chipped beyond saving." She laughed at her own words. "So much for my last two-hundred-dollar manicure and pedicure. And on top of that, I'm covered in sweat and ashes…." She halted her own tirade, remembering how she'd gotten all that ash.

But she wasn't about to put skunk musk on her body, too. "I've done everything you've asked," she stated in a lower tone. "Or…almost everything. And I haven't complained. Not very much. But this is going too far. I can't stand it. I simply refuse."

Hunter let her get it all out. She'd been doing so much better than he had ever imagined she could. It was a miracle that she had held together this far without becoming hysterical. Most women would've demanded to be taken back long ago.

But not Bailey. This daughter of a billionaire, who enjoyed privileges beyond his imagination, was grimy and barely clothed, but her spirit was not broken.

"Okay," he said, and gave in to her. "I'll use some on

myself. It'll take a few minutes for our eyes to become accustomed to the burn, and I'm afraid the scent is even more difficult to get used to. That will take longer. Stand clear now—as far back as possible."

She rolled her eyes. "Go on. We both smell so bad already, this can't be much worse."

He chuckled and turned his back to her in order to spare her the worst of the sting when the musk caught on the breeze. "Don't count on it."

It took about five minutes before their eyes quit tearing and they stopped choking. The smell was harder to stand than he'd remembered.

"Oh, brother," Bailey cried when she could finally speak. "Are you sure this isn't worse than the dog?"

"I'm sure." He shook his head at just the thought of the destruction he had witnessed done by a dog.

"Now, I want to try contacting the Bird People," he told her. "See if I can get them to go back to the Brotherhood for help."

"Who are the Bird People? Where are they?"

Pointing to the sky, he grinned. "The Bird People are our allies in this war with the Skinwalkers. One of my cousins can actually communicate with them. I think they have been following us most of the morning, checking on our welfare."

"Could they help with the dog?"

"No. They're real birds. They don't have superhuman powers or anything unnatural like that. But in the past they've protected us from above when the Skinwalkers changed form into ravens and vultures. Our flying allies wouldn't stand a chance on the ground against a full-size mastiff, though. I'm just hoping they will understand to go for help."

He stepped out to the edge of the granite ledge and threw his voice toward the sky, using the call of a ferruginous hawk. Not exactly sure what he was saying in bird talk, Hunter only hoped it would be understood as a clear cry for assistance.

By the time the sun had passed the midday point and could no longer be seen straight up through the canyon spires, Bailey's tension had grown in equal measure to the heat of the day.

Nothing. For hours they had climbed and scouted every slot canyon and crevice. Still nothing.

Hunter kept asking if she was hungry, but she wasn't. Her body was strung tight, every sense on edge.

At each turn she thought she heard a baby crying. With every small rock slide below their feet, she imagined a massive mongrel was nipping at their heels.

Something had to give soon or she was going to scream.

"It will be twilight before you know it," Hunter said as he stopped to drink from the canteen. "Dusk comes early in these deep canyons. The wind has already died down. Even now it's barely stirring."

His body seemed as tense as hers. "If there is an alternative cave entrance, it's up one of these sheer cliff walls and we're missing it," he mused.

"You're not suggesting that we stop looking! Not when Tara has been alone with those awful people for two days! We can't just give up."

He shook his head. "No. We won't give up. But we're going to have to be a lot more careful during the nighttime hours. Sounds carry easier then. Any noise will give us away."

Hunter pulled his carbine from its place on his pack,

making sure he had it close by. "Keep your ears open for any sound. Anything at all. And find a way to alert me without speaking. Got it?"

This time Bailey nodded silently. As tense as their situation was, he couldn't help grinning at her. He was still surprised and pleased at how very strong and brave his beauty had become.

She grimaced in response to his grin, and then flicked her hand ahead of them with an impatient motion. She obviously didn't want the loss of daylight to slow them down. He knew Bailey had to be feeling shaky. She must be about to collapse from the excesses her body had suffered. Yet she took a deep breath and set her jaw.

As worried as he was about their situation and about how much longer she could keep it up, Hunter discovered his heart fluttering. Not from fear, but from some barely concealed emotion where she was concerned. Though he couldn't acknowledge any of it in the midst of danger.

This was no time to consider what was happening between them. Maybe whatever he felt was based merely on adrenaline and his body's fight for survival.

He turned his back to her and began picking his way along an old sheep path through the canyon. Stopping every few yards to listen, he made sure both of their breathing remained steady and low.

From off in the distance he heard a coyote's bark. It didn't worry him much. A little while later he heard some night birds calling. As dusk settled in around them, he could almost swear he heard the cliffs themselves groaning as they cooled off from the extreme heat of the sun.

He and Bailey were moving along a granite ledge, midway between the canyon floor and the flat mesa above their heads. He strained to listen for any sounds out of place. The hum of a motor. People talking. Anything that would give him a hint of where to look.

Through the purplish haze of twilight settling over the canyons, he finally saw a potential spot for a cave opening. A granite obelisk had, sometime in the past eons of earth movements, been driven straight up from the canyon floor and now lay directly in their path. The rocky sheep path they'd been following split in two around it. The right branch led to the edge of a deep dropoff. Left, the path disappeared into a crevice in the cliff wall that had grown up in brush. Brush that now looked dry from lack of runoff.

He stopped at the split and motioned to Bailey that they should each try a different path. She would take the wider way, around the outside, and he would check out the deep crack in the rock.

She gripped his arm and groaned. Turning back to her, he saw her shaking her head violently.

"No way," she croaked. "Together, or not at all."

Instead of answering, Hunter stood still. He concentrated on listening for any sound that would mean their whereabouts had been given away. And then, as he was about to take another breath, he heard it.

Faint and far-off, the sound of something running. A second later, he could hear panting, too. The dog!

Hunter's blood spiked with life-saving hormones. He pulled Bailey's body around in front of him and shoved her into the dark crevice. Thirty seconds later they came to a blank wall. The end of their road, and most probably the end of their lives.

Without a second's consideration, he pointed past the dry wash of rocks and boulders that had spilled down the shaft with the spring rains. He shoved her toward the brush that had grown up the sheer side of the cliff.

"Up." Knowing it was useless now to be quiet, he roared.

She looked upward, then back at him with pure panic written on her face.

"Go. It's our only chance." He followed her over the slippery boulders and helped her get a sturdy hold on the dried vines clinging to the steep shaft wall. All the while he kept urging her to go faster.

Bailey must have taken a cue from the tension in his voice. Grabbing at the vines and brambles, she scrambled upward as fast as she could and never looked back.

He was right behind her when he heard the dog snarling directly at his heels. Trying to gather his wits enough to climb, while at the same time saying a sacred chant that would protect them from Skinwalkers, Hunter didn't make it.

Fearing this animal was not a Skinwalker, but a real mongrel who would not stop until he brought them down, Hunter let panic snake into his mind.

Snarling, the dog lunged and caught the back of his calf. Jagged teeth tore at the heavy material of his pants and dug into his flesh. Hunter got a firmer handhold on a root sticking out above his head, closed his eyes and concentrated on the chant.

The *yei* were with him this time. As he repeated the ancient words over and over, the pain in his leg began to lessen. With a yip and a snarl, the animal slipped and tumbled backward, over brush and shale.

Hunter didn't miss his opportunity, and quickly moved up inside of the crevice, out of the dog's range. But he was forced to hang tenuously on to roots and rocks as he went. He had no idea how far Bailey had climbed above him, and was nearly nauseated with worry that the terror was not over for them yet. Was this a dog or a Skinwalker? The evidence was still unclear.

As he climbed, the brush thinned out and the crevice walls grew steeper. He became concerned about the roots continuing to hold his weight. Where had Bailey gone?

"Hunter?" A tiny, scared voice reached out to him in the darkness.

Between two giant boulders, a short shelf filled with cactus and weeds slanted back toward the sheer wall. There, Bailey had found a sturdy shelter and waited for him. He shoved aside a creosote bush and swung onto the ledge beside her.

Taking her in his arms, he covered her face with kisses. "You're safe," he groaned, drawing great gulps of air in relief.

She gently pulled out of his arms. "How are we going to get out of here? We can't go back down, and I don't think we can go any higher."

"We're okay for the moment. Take a breath." The shelf was too high and steep for a real dog to reach, but it could still become a death trap for them.

As he should've guessed, it was not a real dog that had chased them up the crevice. And the Skinwalker Dog didn't give them a moment to catch their breaths. Now that Hunter had stopped chanting, the creature roared up the vines toward them, using supernatural powers. The nasty yellow-and-red, crazed eyes gleamed eerily in the darkness as the Dog grew closer.

Hunter shoved Bailey behind him, crouched and drew his rifle. He got off a shot, but missed his moving target. Still, the bullet ricocheted against the steep crevice walls and nicked the Dog's muscular shoulder. Hunter repeated a short, sacred chant.

With a shriek of pain, the Skinwalker Dog fell backward and disappeared into the darkness at the bottom of the shaft. An inhuman stillness filled the night as the echoes of shot and scream faded slowly away in the black void.

"Oh, thank God," Bailey said behind him. "We're safe."

Not so fast, he wanted to caution. But instead, he stood up and took her in his arms. Let her have a moment's peace.

With her nose buried in Hunter's shoulder, Bailey was able to forget about where they were and who was after them. That is, until the sound of voices and shouts penetrated the cocoon of safety he had wrapped around her with his arms.

"Who's that?" she asked. "What are they saying?"

Hunter pursed his lips as a reminder for her to stay silent. They listened to the sounds coming from below, which now seemed like an argument. But the words came up the shaft garbled and indistinct.

Finally, the voices went quiet. He and Bailey stood perfectly still…and waited.

Seconds later, Hunter whispered in her ear. "They may have decided to wait us out. Eventually, we'll need water."

The thought of being trapped up here sent her into a depression unlike any she remembered. This was much more serious than any of her childish blue moods. More serious and much more deadly.

"Bailey, did any of those voices sound familiar?"

"You think it may have been the goons that took Tara and me?"

"Maybe. Probably. But there was another voice I thought I recognized but can't place." Hunter shook his head and tightened his grip around her waist.

He moved to the lip of the shelf and looked down into the black abyss. She couldn't see anything except for a tiny shaft of light coming down the cleft from the stars above.

Hunter pulled her backward, into the shadows away from the edge. "How far back does this shelf go, anyway?"

She shrugged. "I'm supposed to know that?"

As dire as their situation was, Hunter actually chuckled at her words.

"Hold on. I'll check," he told her, and then disappeared in the darkness.

In a second he was back and reaching for her. "There's a slab of granite that was pulled away from the face of the cliff ages ago. It seems to have a deeper shelf around the other side. That could be safer, and it might even provide us with a way to climb out of this crevice. But we'd have to jump a two- or three-foot-wide crack in the shelf to get there."

"I don't think I can." Every nerve was strung tight and she was already shaking like a leaf. What more could she stand?

"Take it easy," he said. Reaching out, he used his thumb to stroke her chin. "I'll help you. You've already done things I didn't think you could do. I've been really impressed. Don't quit on me now. I need you to be strong just a little longer."

She took a deep breath and tried not to cry. "I don't—"

A sudden noise from below interrupted her words. Hunter stepped to the edge and looked over.

"They're starting a fire. Trying to kill us with the smoke, or at least to block any possible escape route."

"Ohmigod." Her knees grew weak again and she clung to him in fright. Fire.

"We have to jump for the other side now for sure. This shaft we're in will act like a chimney. The flames may or may not kill us here, but smoke inhalation definitely will."

"Uh…" She was paralyzed, near hysteria.

"Trust me, Bailey," he said as he shoved her ahead of him into the blackness at the back of the shelf. "And when I say jump, bend you knees and go. I'll be right behind you."

Hunter was grateful that Bailey seemed to be staying so strong. At the last moment, he'd taken her hand and gone with her. Together they'd landed on a bigger shelf, in a much narrower shaft that seemed to go straight up.

Now, he was urging her to move as far back as possible into this darker slot. He couldn't help but worry about extreme heat and the real potential for lack of oxygen in the narrower shaft. Sheltering her body with his own, he quickly ripped a strip from his shirt and wet it with canteen water.

"Here," he said as he handed her the cloth. "Keep this over your mouth."

She whimpered, but took it.

As his eyes grew more accustomed to the darkness, Hunter realized they had entered a new, smaller shaft and that the granite outcropping in the cliff would probably protect them from direct flames. But he knew it offered little protection from the smoke and the heat.

"Keep inching farther into the shaft. As far as you can go," he urged.

Hunter poured half the remaining water in the canteen over Bailey's head and splashed the rest over his own. Just as he finished, he heard the roar of flames starting up the main shaft behind them.

Bailey sobbed and pushed herself deeper into the narrowing slot. He tried to follow, but discovered the backpack wouldn't fit. Turning to shrug it off, he felt a gust of heat on his face and shut his eyes against the scorching blast.

He swung around and shoved his body up tightly against Bailey's back, trying desperately to protect her. The roar of the fire deafened him, but he swore he heard her cry out.

Was this going to be their end?

Then he felt her grabbing the front of his shirt and trying to drag him closer. She tugged, and he managed to squeeze his face farther into the narrow opening.

As she pulled and he inched farther into the increasingly tighter space, he noticed the shirt on his back growing hotter. He wasn't too sure what he could do if it suddenly burst into flames. Hating to think what would happen to Bailey if he became a human torch, Hunter began to murmur a ceremonial song of protection for her.

Just then, he felt cool air touch his face. A draft of oxygen was coming from somewhere in front of him, pulled toward the fire that was running up the other shaft.

He'd moved as far into the opening in the rock as he could go, but his rear was still exposed. At least Bailey had a chance of making it.

Closing his mind to the fire and its potential consequences, he stood stoically as his back took the brunt of the heat. If he lived through this, he would find that Skinwalker Dog and kill it—along with the two goons, who were too stupid to live. And he would see the baby reunited with its mother no matter how difficult that task turned out to be.

But as he slowly lost consciousness, and his spirit began melting with the heat, his mind turned to Bailey. If he lived, he had no idea what to do about her.

She was passion and she was poison.

Nope. He had absolutely no idea what to do at all.

Chapter 8

Their hiding place in the dark shaft had been silent, with no lingering sounds of the crackling fire, for what seemed like hours. Bailey opened her eyes and took a deep breath of the cool, life-giving air coming from the crevice before her. Her nose was buried as deep as possible in the tiny opening.

She could feel Hunter still jammed tightly against her back. But he was so quiet. So deathly quiet.

"Hunter?"

He didn't make a sound. Did that mean he wanted her to keep quiet, too, so as not to give away their position?

Suddenly panicked, she twisted around and faced his chest. Nudging him slightly in complete silence, she expected him to give her a sign in return, indicating things were okay.

Instead, his whole body crumbled where he stood. He went down backward in a heap on their narrow ledge.

Gasping, she knelt beside him and looked around. Everything was dark. There didn't seem to be any flames remaining in the shaft, just a few glowing embers here and there. But her nostrils were still assailed with the stench of smoke and ash.

She touched Hunter's cheek, and her throat closed with dryness and fear, plus the bitter, choking taste of charcoal. Crying softly, she bent to croak in his ear. "Can you hear me? Please don't be dead."

He made no sound. No movement at all.

Tendrils of pure hysteria reached out, grabbed at her chest and punched at her stomach. What would she do? How would she get out of here?

Looking down into his beautiful, blackened face in the starlight, Bailey realized it really didn't matter. If Hunter never left this shaft alive, then she didn't want to, either.

It was a huge revelation. One she hoped she wouldn't have a lot of time to consider. If their end was near, let it come fast.

At that moment, a strange bird call sounded down the rock chimney, a singsong whistle that almost scared her to death. Looking up the shaft, she saw the outline of something large bending over the edge of the mesa, staring down the cleft and blocking out most of the starlight.

Skinwalkers! Where the heck was Hunter's gun? She crawled around his body, searching frantically in the dark for his rifle. Those damn Skinwalkers would not get away with killing them so easily. Not if she still had the strength to pull a trigger.

One more spine-tingling call reached her ears just as her fingers touched hot metal. "Ow!" She couldn't stop her yelp of pain.

"Cousin?" A man's soft call echoed down the shaft. "Ms. Howard?"

"Huh? Who is it?" She coughed and fought for air. Her throat was clogged with fear and emotion, along with plenty of thick, black soot.

"Stay where you are. I'll come for you." The deep masculine voice did not sound threatening, but chills of alarm ran along her spine.

Bailey forgot the probably useless rifle and gave up on the idea of killing anyone. She turned and crawled back to Hunter's inert body. She leaned her cheek on his chest so that her body was covering and protecting his. If this was a trick and the Skinwalkers attacked them down here, she didn't want to look at the bastards as they took their lives. Let them stab her in the back and get it over with.

But as her own thudding heart began to calm, she heard another stronger beat coming from under her ear. Hunter's life was not yet lost. And Bailey vowed that if it came to the ultimate, she would gladly give up her life to save his.

She heard heavy breathing behind her as someone or some *thing* reached their small, dark shelf. A beam of light clicked on and ran an eerie glow over both her and Hunter.

"Ms. Howard? It's all right. I am Lucas Tso, a cousin of Hunter Long's. I have…"

Hunter stirred, lifted his head and rested his body on his elbows. "Where…" His words choked off as he began coughing and wheezing.

Bailey sat up beside him. "Hunter. My God. Are you okay?" Her own words were squeaky and hoarse.

She didn't know what to do to help him while he was racked with horrific spasms of coughing and gasping. She dug her fingers into his shirt and tried to help him breathe by holding him upright. But her efforts seemed useless.

Gentle hands came from behind and pulled her away from Hunter. "Let me see if there's something I can do."

A dark form of a man knelt beside Hunter's body and began soft chanting. There was enough light for her to realize that he also was easing a canteen to Hunter's lips and helping him take small swallows between gasps.

"Quiet," the stranger said soothingly to Hunter. "Do not try to speak until you are out of this smoke-saturated shaft. I can understand your meaning without the words. It was smart of you to start a fire so we could spot this cleft in the mesa. The smoke was visible for many miles, but—"

"No!" The man interrupted himself as he gripped Hunter by the shoulder and tried to make him stay still. "You will be first, the woman next. Calm down, cousin. Let me help you find the harmony in your body."

In a few moments, Hunter's coughs had lessened to wheezing, and Bailey felt her own tension begin to ease.

The stranger stopped chanting and turned to her. "Ms. Howard. I'm a member of the Brotherhood and we've been searching for you two for most of the day. The Bird People led us to the area, but we had trouble finding you until we smelled smoke. Now Hunter will not participate in his own healing until you have taken at least a sip of water."

Lucas handed her the canteen. She took one gulp of cool water and began to spit up.

"Sorry," Hunter's cousin said as he took back the canteen. "We must get you both out of here so your lungs can breathe in healing fresh air. I'll help you climb up the rope. My cousin refuses to go until you are safe."

"Rope?" she managed to ask with a rasp.

"Don't worry. I can carry you. It'll be okay...."

"I can't leave without Hunter." She was crying past the hoarseness and the fear. "Take him. I'll wait."

Bailey was prepared to stand her ground and refuse to go without seeing Hunter to safety first. But then her old college lover reached out in the darkness and took her hand. His big, warm fingers squeezed hers. She felt the connection, knowing immediately what he was trying to say.

"Please." She was whining, and even in the dark she could see Hunter wince. "I'm okay, really. You go ahead."

He tightened his grip in stern silence, and she understood her continued refusal would be a lost cause.

"Come now," the cousin told her gently as he tugged on her shoulder. "If you can relax, it will only take a few minutes to get you to safety. The faster we go up, the faster I can come back down for him."

"I can relax," she said softly. It was the one thing Bailey had learned she was capable of doing to help. Though it didn't seem like much of an accomplishment.

Hunter's cousin had not been lying. After a short time spent over his shoulder, she found herself sitting on solid ground and dragging in huge gulps of life-saving fresh air.

"You will be safe here with me until our cousin can bring up Hunter Long," a different stranger said, bending over her and holding out a canteen. "I'm Michael Ayze. I'm also a member of the Brotherhood and another of Hunter's relatives. Try taking deep breaths and small sips of water."

Bailey wasn't frightened. She also wasn't going to take a sip, or anything else, for that matter, until she was sure Hunter was safe.

She turned her head just as Lucas disappeared back down into the still-smoldering slash in the flat ground, their personal chimney shaft in the mountain. Going onto all fours, she tried to crawl over to the edge. But after one small, halting advance of her body, everything went suddenly dark. She slipped away into a comfortable unconsciousness.

Hunter had finally found his voice again, though it might take him days to lose the raspiness when trying to talk. He'd coughed up enough black stuff in the last hour to make him positive cigarettes would never be a temptation in his lifetime.

They were all up on top of the mesa, under a small clump of juniper trees. The group could stay here in relative safety as his two cousins gave him and Bailey some time to recover before they went after the baby.

His cousin Michael had administered a short healing rite to help him clear his lungs, and was now mixing medicines with water to give to Bailey. Lucas had plastered Hunter's blistered back with soothing salve before he went off to scout the area.

Nothing could be done to make Hunter's singed hair look any better. But luckily, his rifle had cooled off and wasn't cooked, and the backpack was sooty but still in one piece.

Bailey had been resting with her head in his lap for the last fifteen minutes. Her short, sudden blackout before he was rescued had turned out to be residual exhaustion and lack of oxygen. They knew she needed sleep more than anything else to help her body recover. But they couldn't give her very much time.

Hunter was absolutely amazed how, despite everything she had been through, she still hung in there with him. The tension that had kept him so strung up for the last few days should begin loosening its grip now that his cousins had arrived.

They could take Bailey to safety. She would be all right. He watched as Lucas moved in from the shadows, returning to where they lay hidden under a few juniper and piñon trees. His cousin had been looking for the Skinwalkers or any sign of the baby.

"Did you find anything?" he asked in a raspy whisper.

Lucas came closer so he, too, could keep his voice low. "The Skinwalkers must believe you two are dead, because most of them have left the area. But the Skinwalker Dog you saw took no chances. He posted one of his goons at the bottom of the crevice, even though the vines and brush you climbed have burned away, and there is no possibility of anyone getting down that way. They seem unaware or unconcerned that there is a shelf and footholds to climb up the inside of the shaft to this mesa."

Hunter smiled in the dark. The hired Navajo henchmen he'd seen were not Skinwalkers and didn't have any of their powers. One normal human would be easy to overpower if necessary, and such a man would undoubtedly not be bright enough to find his way up to the top of the cleft.

"Before you started after us," he began, "had you heard the reasons for taking the child? Is a ransom to be paid?"

Lucas lowered his voice even more. "The Concho family is rich, but money is not what the kidnappers are after. Your brother went to the Concho ranch shortly after you began tracking. Old Hastiin Willie claims he has something special the Navajo Wolf is after.

"He wouldn't say what, but Kody convinced him to let us protect his property with a special ceremony using some of the chants Shirley Nez's uncle found in those parchments before he died."

Hunter nodded, but winced internally at the mention of Shirley Nez. He missed the Brotherhood's old mentor and wished she was still alive to give them advice.

"Willie Concho seems to know all about this new Navajo Wolf—and about the Brotherhood."

"Which side is he on?"

"The winning side, would've been my best guess." Lucas smiled wryly. "That is, until his granddaughter was kidnapped."

Hunter tried to focus on their objective. "While you were out did you see any sign of a hidden cave entrance? Or hear any baby's cries?"

Lucas shook his head. "I saw a couple of possibilities, but have not yet had a chance to scout them. I wanted to check on your condition first."

Hunter bristled, but quickly reminded himself of the value of harmony and balance. "I am fine."

"And the woman?"

That was a question he found harder to answer. "I believe she will be fine, as well. Though she needs to go back to civilization. Her body is strong, but her harmony is fragile. She requires a sing and should—"

Bailey opened her eyes and lifted her head. "If you're talking about me, I'm doing okay. Good enough to help rescue Tara. I intend to stay."

He wanted to demand she do as he said, but knew it wouldn't be smart in her condition. "That would not be wise," he muttered instead.

"Well, nobody ever said I was the brightest kid on the block. I've done lots of things in my life that weren't exactly brilliant. But this one is important. So I'm sticking with it until it's over." She sat up and crossed her legs.

Her straight back and set jaw clearly said she had made up her mind. Hunter sighed and rolled his eyes.

He gave up for the moment and turned to his cousin.

"After you rest for a while, will you and Michael continue searching for another way to the Skinwalker cave? There was cool air in our faces on that narrow shelf. I believe that must mean the source of the fresh air is from a deep cavern. Maybe the *right* cavern."

"We will search. But as we do, both you and Ms. Howard must sleep. You will be no help to the child if you're dead on your feet."

Hunter nodded and turned to Bailey. "That meet with your approval, slick?"

She screwed up her mouth as if she tasted something sour. "I'm not sure I can sleep. I'm too tense."

"You will sleep," Lucas told her. "And you will be able to help when the time comes. Don't let your secret doubts turn you away from the harmony that's inside you."

Bailey looked at him as if he had suddenly grown wings. Hunter couldn't keep the smile from spreading across his face. He took her hand and silently let their connection give her strength. The force between them was still powerful and electrifying.

He would get her through this by sheer determination.

She woke up alone, lying on her folded arms under Hunter's space-age-material blanket. She must've been asleep for a couple of hours. As Bailey rubbed her eyes and sat up, she realized that the gray, predawn light had begun to illuminate the mesa where they'd spent the night.

Glancing around for Hunter, she discovered he hadn't gone far. Just over to the east rim of the mesa, to face the rising crimson glow. He was chanting dawn prayers.

As he finished throwing bits of pollen into the air, and repacked his supplies in the medicine pouch, Bailey looked about in the growing light. What a strange place this was. It seemed at first glance like a flat desert, with bits of shrubs and short evergreens sticking up like green birthday candles on a dull beige cake.

The most amazing thing, though, was the existence of the disappearing canyons. She knew the narrow shafts were right below her. But sitting here on the mesa surface and looking out, you'd never guess the steep-sided gashes were even there until you came to the very edge and looked down. It would be easy to run right over the side of a hundred-foot dropoff if you weren't paying careful attention.

Hunter came back to squat beside her, his familiar grin plastered in place. "How are you feeling? Hungry?"

She frowned. "Everything hurts, and I told you I don't eat in the morning."

"You must drink water."

"Yeah. Yeah. Give me the canteen." She was getting crankier and crankier. But damn it, her body was sore, her clothes were a wreck and she needed a hairdresser and a candy bar in the worst way.

Taking a sip of the metallic-tasting water, she remembered why she wasn't at home or at some nearby resort or spa. *Tara.* The biggest reason she had not gotten out of this godforsaken wilderness when she'd first had the opportunity. The baby was worth all the discomfort.

Then she looked into the sexy, stormy eyes of the man beside her, who was currently studying her face. He was arrogant and frustrating most of the time, but she owed him her life. And now she owed him her heart. He was also worth every bit of what she'd been through.

"Have you changed your mind about letting one of my cousins take you back to your father while we keep looking for the baby? Michael Ayze has a Jeep hidden in a wash a few miles away." Hunter's voice was a raspy whisper.

"Not on your life, bud." She tried to get to her feet, but overbalanced with the canteen in her hand, and slipped back down on her rear end. "I haven't been through everything so far just to walk away right before we rescue Tara. Nuh-uh. Not happening. Forget about it."

Hunter eased to his feet and helped her get up. "I'm a Tribal Police special investigator. I could insist you go, or else have you locked up when we get back."

It was her turn to roll her eyes. "Don't be such a jerk. You know I have to see this through. Stop bugging me about going back."

He heaved a heavy, put-upon sigh and made her chuckle.

Bailey wanted to change the subject. "Tell me about your cousins," she asked, while handing him back the canteen. "They're both yummy looking, but they seem pretty stoic. What's their background and how come they belong to this Brotherhood deal? In fact, why do you belong?"

He took a sip and then gazed out at the lavender-shaded mountains visible to the north, in what must be either Utah or Colorado. "When I was a kid, I spent summers with the family of my mother's uncle, as a shepherd. My great-uncle, Hastiin Raymond Gashie, found time to teach me the Navajo Way, along with lessons on how to track. He wanted me to appreciate who I am in relation to the People and to the world around me."

Bailey put away the canteen and kicked out the cricks and cramps from hours spent lying on the hard ground. Hunter turned to watch her, grinned then held out his hand again.

"Come look at the beauty of this morning," he said.

Going to his side, she took the offered hand. Immediately she felt warmth, electricity and awe in nearly equal measures. Standing by his side gave her the strangest feeling. True companionship, perhaps? That was something she knew very little about, so maybe that was it.

She wanted to be his friend—and his lover. But this feeling was something more undefined and special.

"The view is spectacular," she told him truthfully. It was one of the most amazing sights she had ever beheld.

Morning sun shone down on the valley, causing the rich red earth to glow. To the west, stark gray monoliths rose like lonely sentinels out of the orange-colored sand. In between, across the floor of the valley, enough plant life grew to add a whimsical touch of green and silver to the landscape.

What she was seeing surely must be what poets meant when they used the word *splendor.*

"Few outsiders ever get to see this sight," Hunter told her without changing the direction of his gaze. "When I was a kid, my uncle taught me to pay attention to places. To really see what your eyes could show you, and to memorize it so you can bring the places back to your mind when you need them.

"More than that," Hunter continued, "my uncle felt a Navajo should walk the ground, touch the stones, smell the cedar and breathe the desert dust. He taught me to enjoy a rare summer rain, watch a mother prairie dog feed her young and listen to the rocks as they speak to us in the wind."

Bailey was fascinated. The man was a poet, along with being an advocate for nature. Who would've thought?

Hunter turned to gaze into her eyes. For a moment it seemed as though he was still looking at the spectacular vista, because his face carried that awed expression. But he was staring directly at her with those brilliant eyes.

He shook his head lightly and smiled. "Sorry, what I meant to say is Dinetah is a part of who we are as Navajos. The land is in our bones and buried in our spirits. It is our religion and our family. There's supposed to be a balance in nature, and the Dine learn early how to follow in that same stream of harmony.

"The harmony between the sacred four mountains is in danger now. Skinwalkers are working to destroy the balance we usually manage to maintain with little effort. But there are some of us who will not allow that to happen. My cousins and I risk all to fight off the evil. We do so because it is part of who we are."

He dropped her hand and went to spread out the blanket under the tree. "Sit and rest for a few more minutes. Michael and Lucas will be back soon, and then we'll have to go."

She did as he suggested and waited until he joined her there.

"My cousin Michael is a brilliant man, an expert in anthropology," Hunter told her when they were settled. "He was a professor at Yale University. But when he heard about the Skinwalker terror in Dinetah, he came back to do what he could to help. Now he teaches part-time at the Dine College and says it was a mistake for him to ever walk away from Navajoland."

Bailey thought of the big burly man with kind eyes, and was surprised to know he was a professor. But when she considered it further, she realized what she had been seeing was superintelligence shining from those eyes.

"My cousin Lucas is another story."

"Oh, yeah. He's nice but, um, strange?"

"Not really all that strange," Hunter hedged. "He's a 'sensitive.' One who hears others' thoughts and can sometimes see the future. He's been a tremendous help to the Brotherhood. In fact, Lucas Tso is an uncommon man in many ways. Besides those gifts, he's also a famous silversmith. His jewelry and paintings have been shown in galleries all over the world. He's been a medal-winning, iron-man triathlete, and no one on the reservation would stand a chance against him in a footrace."

"Can he really hear people's thoughts?"

Hunter laughed. "Don't worry. He would never pry into your secrets or dreams."

A long, shrill whistle broke the dawn air. Hunter touched a hand to her arm in order to calm her fears, and a moment later Michael and Lucas appeared, seemingly out of nowhere.

"We found another way into the cavern, cousin," Michael said when he came close. "But we're going to have to move fast if we are to rescue the child."

"I have heard the thoughts of the Skinwalker Dog," Lucas added. "We must stop what is happening. Now. Before it is forever too late to help the little girl."

Chapter 9

Bailey sat on the piñon needles back in the old coyote cave, fuming and choking down another MRE. Hunter and Lucas had gone off to rescue the baby, and she and Michael were stuck here together, waiting for them to return.

"I don't understand," she said past the dry paste that was gluing itself to the roof of her mouth. "Did they have to go all the way to the San Juan River? Is that how they planned to sneak into the cave?"

Michael was sitting Indian-style beside the fire pit. He turned those warm, intelligent eyes her way.

"The San Juan isn't far, and it's extremely low this year due to the drought. You may never have seen the beauty of the river when it was in its glory." His brown eyes took on a wistful dreaminess. "But not too long ago, crystal-blue waters snaked around golden sandstone buttes streaked with desert varnish—uh, those are mineral deposits that look like burnt chocolate.

"Still today," he continued with a sigh, "it's a magical, ancient place laced with hidden pictographs and cool grottos. Not as sacred to the People as Canyon de Chelly, certainly. But water means life in the desert, so the river is a part of what it means to be Dine."

Michael shifted and smiled. "I know that wasn't what you asked, but I become a teacher at every opportunity. My cousins did not go to the river because the water level is so low. Much of the long-lost landscape is now revealed, and every crevice is wide open. It would be impossible for us to find a way into the Skinwalker cavern from that direction without being spotted.

"But Lucas Tso and I uncovered what is probably one of the big cavern's smaller tributaries. Actually, the opening we found is quite near the chimney shaft where you and Hunter were nearly burned alive."

Michael hesitated after speaking those graphic words, then continued. "This smaller entrance we found could be called a back door into the huge main chamber of the cavern. Hunter had been certain such a thing must exist, because you heard the baby's cries and he felt the fresh air. And he was right."

"But if it's a back door, why couldn't we all go? Why are you stuck babysitting me while Hunter and Lucas go to get Tara?"

"You're a bright woman. You must realize that Hunter would not be in top form as long as he was worried about your welfare. He might make mistakes—mistakes that could cost someone's life."

She almost opened her mouth to deny that Hunter gave

a damn about her welfare. After all, he had never said he cared. That's what had broken them up years earlier, and today very little had changed where he was concerned. He was still the closemouthed charmer he'd always been and probably always would be.

But it would sound too ungrateful and childish, even to herself. He had saved her life, several times.

So she said the next thing that was waiting to jump out of her mouth. "Does Hunter date lots of women? Do you know if he's ever been married?"

"Don't you think those questions would be better asked of my cousin himself?"

"Hunter would never answer me straight out. The man is infuriating. My life is an open book—literally. And I know so very little about him."

The corners of Michael's mouth tipped up in the semblance of a smile. "Yes, even I read in a magazine that you were married once a while ago. How long did the union last?"

She waved her hand dismissively, no longer embarrassed by the question. She'd heard it enough times to have a dozen snappy comebacks ready. This time she picked the simple truth.

"Forty-seven hours and twenty minutes. My father's lawyers had the marriage annulled. Thank goodness."

"You didn't love the man?"

"Hell, no. I was drunk out of my mind. It would've been a terrible mistake to stay with him. He was a worse drinker than I was back then. And a movie stuntman to boot. I can't imagine any more terrible combination than danger and alcohol." She shook her head. "Two years after I last saw him, I heard he'd been crippled in a stunt. My guess is he was drunk that time, too."

"Then why did you marry him?"

It was a fair question. But one she didn't intend to answer. It had taken her years of therapy to understand that her ex-husband's looks, his long mahogany hair and gray eyes, had reminded her of Hunter. In a booze- and drug-filled haze, she'd picked a guy who looked like the man she had always wanted and could never have.

"Just a drunken stunt of my own," she told his cousin instead.

Michael's expression softened. "People are rarely so honest. Thank you."

She shrugged. "You might as well know that I'm also a drug addict. But I've been to rehab. I'm cured."

"I was under the impression that addicts have no cure in the Anglo world. One slip and you'll return to your demons. Isn't that so?"

"I'm cured. In my case it's over."

For a few moments Michael studied her face in the soft afternoon light coming from the cave entrance. She could tell he thought she was deluding herself by believing she was completely cured. But he didn't say it.

Instead, he asked a question. "I think I've also heard that you spent your childhood summers in Dinetah with your grandmother. True?"

Bailey nodded. "But for just a few weeks at a time. That is, until the two summers I was in college. Then I stayed longer, to spend the time with Hunter."

"But if she was like most Dine grandmothers," Michael said with a wide smile, "I'd imagine she couldn't resist giving you lessons on being Navajo."

Laughing, Bailey remembered all the legends and

stories she'd been told. "I think being Navajo must mean you can't stop yourself from talking too much."

"You are also Navajo. Aren't you?"

"Yes, but…" She *was* Navajo. And though that side would not consider it special, her Anglo side was proud of it. But she hadn't bothered to think about being Navajo in such a way before. Maybe that's why she always had too much to say in every situation.

Michael smiled again. "Hunter Long has never married," he told her, in a change of subject she welcomed. "But he hasn't talked to me about why not."

Shifting, he raised his eyebrows in thought. "In the Brotherhood we each have a…well, I guess you would call it a specialty. We don't speak of it, but each of us is better at some things than the others."

"What's Hunter's thing?" she asked, interrupting him.

"I call him the 'muscle,'" Michael said with a chuckle. "He never stops moving. He's constantly searching for the evil ones, and when it comes down to a battle with the Skinwalkers, Hunter is the first one to draw his knife."

Yes, that sounded like Hunter, though she didn't want to think of him in any battles. "What's your specialty?" she asked Michael.

"I'm the brains of the outfit." He shrugged a shoulder. "I know that with this build I don't look like I'm terribly smart. But I am one to think things through carefully before I make any moves. Perhaps I sometimes spend far too long thinking."

He barked a laugh at his own expense and then continued. "My cousin Hunter has a lot of anger inside him. Too much to stand still or to try being reasonable. It's easy to read the anger in the way he reacts."

"But he smiles all the time," she argued. "And he can be so gentle and charming."

"Yes, I agree with you. The anger seems at war with who he really is."

"Why do you think he's that way? What's he got to be angry about?"

"I have no idea. But I'm convinced that's why he's never had a serious relationship with a woman. The anger scares him sometimes."

Bailey had to think about what Michael said. Really think about it. Why would Hunter have all that pent-up anger? His childhood? Maybe.

"Don't be so nervous and upset over the Skinwalkers possibly hurting Hunter or the baby. I can guarantee it will be okay."

"Excuse me?"

Michael pointed to her hands. Looking down, she found herself rubbing them together nervously. Wringing her hands? She must need that chocolate bar far worse than she'd imagined.

Stopping her jerky, unconscious movements, she forced herself to quietly fold her hands in her lap. "I'm okay."

"My cousins will be back soon with the child." Michael's voice was soothing. "Everything will be all right. The Brotherhood has been gifted with a few sacred chants that can keep the Skinwalkers at bay. So far, it's been our best defense when they come after us."

"Maybe you need a better offense."

He chuckled again and nodded. "I'm working on it. If we can hold off the attacks long enough to allow us to keep looking for the answers, I know we'll find them. It's only a matter of time."

Shifting, he stood. "I'm going to stand lookout at the cave entrance. Can you sleep for awhile?"

She shook her head, but knew there weren't many choices. "I'll try to rest. Thanks."

Positive she could not will her eyes to close nor her brain to stop whirling, Bailey lay back and stared at the fire. There couldn't be any rest for her until Hunter and Tara were sitting right here beside her and they all were truly safe from the Skinwalkers.

The Skinwalker Dog was currently in his human persona, and sweating like a pig. Running his forefinger between his neck and his too-tight collar, he picked up a cell phone and called his boss.

He needed to be extremely careful during this particular conversation with the Navajo Wolf. If he said too much, or accidently expressed something the wrong way, he would likely be dead before the sun came up tomorrow.

Greeting the Wolf cordially, the Dog started with his best news. "I have the map in my hands. Willie Concho delivered it exactly as he was instructed. We found no evidence that he'd brought the FBI or anyone else with him, either."

After a second's silence, the Wolf replied, "Is the map in good shape? Are the markings still readable after all these centuries?"

"I've only given it a quick glance. Seems okay to me, though."

"Good. Excellent. And the child?"

"We did like you told us and used a doll for the trade-off with Concho. If the FBI or anyone else had stopped our exchange, we still would've had the baby to deal with. But since we've got the map now, what do you want us to do with the kid? She's starting to be a big liability."

"There should be no violence, but she cannot leave the desert. Find a way to quietly get rid of both the kid and the old caretaker woman we hired."

"I understand. I've got an isolated cabin in mind. Their end will come as peacefully as possible. No sweat."

"Fine. Then bring the map to—"

"There is one small loose end. Or I should say, there could be a loose end."

"Your hesitation might be an extremely dangerous mistake for you." The sentence was uttered in a threatening growl. The Dog cringed in response.

This was the tricky part, trying to lie to the Navajo Wolf in order to give himself an opportunity to hide the map. Originally, the Dog had been terrified at the very idea. But if it worked, he would have riches beyond imagining.

If it didn't work, he would never have anything again.

On the other end of the phone, the Wolf clearly heard the lie in the Dog's voice, and decided he'd better listen carefully. The Wolf was well aware that one of the most difficult things about heading up a cult of Skinwalkers was the treachery that grew among the greedy bastards. But their deceptions were minor and usually didn't matter. Nothing mattered now that he had the map.

If the Dog dared lie about anything to do with the ancient map that would lead to the parchments, however, the cur's throat would be cut within hours.

The Dog had been a good lieutenant, a decent right-hand man. But he might end up being too smart for his own good. Perhaps he should start counting the breaths of air remaining in his time on earth. The countdown to his end had already begun, regardless of the reasons for his lies.

"The woman we kidnapped with the child was not the baby's mother," the Dog told him, with great respect clearly ringing in his voice. "That mistake has now been avenged. The man most responsible for taking the wrong woman will never see daylight again. And his partner learned a good lesson. One he won't soon forget as he works with a new man."

"Who was she?" The Wolf had a feeling this conversation was going to cost him something.

"The daughter of a rich man. We missed an opportunity with that one."

Dismissing the thought, the Wolf waited for the rest of the lies. "Money was never the point. The map is in our hands now, isn't it?"

"Yeah, sure. But it gets worse. Seems the Brotherhood took an interest in our operation. They sent a man, a tracker I know well. But I never knew of his connection to them."

"Who is this man?"

"He was a Navajo Tribal Police special investigator by the name of Hunter Long. But he and the woman are both now dead."

The name seemed vaguely familiar to the Wolf. But it must have been a very distant link, for he couldn't bring the memory to the forefront of his mind. Lately, the white powder he'd been using to turn into the Wolf seemed to be interfering more and more with his memory.

He'd been planning ahead for the desperate battle with the ancient sickness he knew inevitably came to Skinwalkers. Hoping to find a way around the illness before the old, painful death overcame them all, the Wolf had become convinced the parchments would provide the answer. And the map would tell them where to find the parchments.

For now, the effort to remember the tribal policeman's image left him cold and nauseated. But this man could not be important in the larger scheme of things if he was already dead. The Wolf vowed to quickly forget the name and never try to think of it again.

"If you're sure the policeman and the woman are dead, why are you mentioning them?" he grumbled with irritation. "Just bring me the map and do what you're told."

"There is some evidence that other Brotherhood members have entered the territory. Perhaps looking for the baby. Perhaps to look for their dead comrade."

"That was not part of our plan. You are failing, Dog." The Wolf grew more and more annoyed. "Do not bother me with these details. Just get into one of the helicopters and meet me with the map as you agreed. Stop talking about changes in the plan on an unsecure phone line."

"Oh, no one will know about all this except you and me. But I need a little time. Before I can meet with you, I have to be sure I'm not being followed by the Brotherhood. In fact, this might be a terrific opportunity to kill off a few more of those secretive do-gooders."

"I want that map. Avoid the Brotherhood and bring it to me."

"Just a few hours," the Dog pleaded. "I must be sure the Brotherhood doesn't catch us while we're stashing the baby."

"Don't you have anyone you can trust to take care of the baby? I insist you do as I say. You can't let that map out of your sight. Surely any soldier could deal with a kid and an old lady?"

"It's too dangerous." The Dog continued on with his argument. "The map might be lost if I'm ambushed."

"What did you say?" The Wolf's mind was reeling. He couldn't keep up with the Dog's fast talking as long as his head pounded this way. How could it be so hard to think?

"Twelve more hours. That's all I ask," the Dog said hurriedly. "Give me the time and soon enough you will be holding the map in your hands."

Holding the map in your hands. That was all the Wolf needed to hear. He quickly agreed to the request, hung up the phone and went to fix himself another batch of the powder.

The Dog was a dead man walking. Let him bring the map. After that, his usefulness would be over.

Hunter could feel the cool draft of air on his face, but the tiny black hole in the cleft Lucas was pointing out seemed too tight for either of them to get through. He was having trouble concentrating on their goal. All he seemed able to think about was Bailey, and whether or not she was safe with Michael.

"The woman is safe enough, cousin," Lucas whispered.

Hunter hadn't said a word, but his cousin had known his thoughts. Bailey was right when she'd said he was a little strange.

"We'll have to break through the rock around the hole to widen the opening," Lucas told him. "But the shale has thinned here from a million years of dripping rainwater. It shouldn't be too difficult."

"Do you think they'll hear us breaking in?"

Lucas shook his head. "Keep trying to find your balance. The harmony in your spirit will allow you to remain silent."

Hunter bit back a sarcastic remark he didn't want to say.

He knew damn well he was in need of a curing ceremony to restore his balance. But it was unlikely, even after he regained the full harmony that would come from a sing, that he could be quiet enough. These were Skinwalkers they were dealing with.

Lucas put a hand on his chest in order to slow him down. "Listen to my words and to my voice. It is your anger that keeps you from finding balance, not the woman."

Well, that was just nonsense. He respected Lucas, but his cousin was suddenly spouting idiotic statements with no reason.

Hunter knew he kept old anger inside him like a boy-hood friend. But he'd done that ever since he could re-member. This new, stronger loss of harmony he was feeling had to be coming from conflicted feelings about Bailey. She must be the one who was making his emotions spin and his world tilt.

He regretted the eight years they'd wasted. The years when he could've helped her find her balance, and perhaps found his own, too. Instead, he'd struggled through his angry life and allowed her to make all the wrong turns. He'd been an ass.

And now it was far too late for any of that. She'd already found her way to harmony. All she needed was a little shove from her Navajo side to let her see it. It was too late for him to help her—or himself.

Once they were out of danger and she had been through a ceremony, she would go back to her family and her life as a changed woman. Hunter could see she had been coming to an understanding of who she was. With a ceremony to put her spirit back into balance, she truly would be cured of her addictive demons, and in harmony with her spirit.

She wouldn't need him for anything anymore.

"Force your mind to clear," Lucas demanded quietly. "Right now, you must stay in the moment. Later we will talk about demons. Yours and hers."

"Mine?"

"I have seen your father in a dream. I have seen him as the Navajo Wolf."

"That's impossible. My father has been dead for years." But Hunter had dreamed the same thing. Many times.

"Keep your spirit still for now and concentrate. Later, when the child is safe, we will talk about dreams."

Hunter turned and kicked at the rock around the narrow opening. As the limestone and shale began to break away, he smelled more cool air—a breeze that must be coming from a large underground space. This had to be the way in they'd searched for.

As soon as the opening was wide enough for a man to squeeze through, the cousins scrambled downward into the darkness. Lucas flicked a small flashlight's beam around the area where they stood.

Hunter discovered they were standing in a steep shale tunnel that headed down into an ever-widening cave. Michael had talked to him once about how many centuries' worth of erosion it took to make one of these huge underground spaces. Cavern formation made for a fascinating study.

But right now Hunter was more interested in the flow of air past his body. If they followed the currents, they would find another entrance to this cavity, he was positive. Air didn't simply flow from nowhere. Likely a cave opening onto the San Juan river would be the source. And somewhere en route was where the baby was being held.

Lucas bent his head and began silently shuffling down

the dark corridor, periodically flipping the flashlight beam above and below. Hunter followed on his heels.

They moved that way for what seemed like a long time. Every once in a while one of them would slip on loose rocks, but be saved from falling by the other one. They worked well together, and in total silence.

As the path finally began to flatten out, Hunter heard the unmistakable sound of a baby. Not crying, but talking and laughing in that garbled way of a toddler.

Those might just be the best sounds he had ever heard.

The closer they came to the source of the sounds, the slower the two cousins moved. Soon, light spreading through the cavern made the flashlight unnecessary. When they heard the old grandmother making gentle sounds of her own, each man took a deep breath.

So far the child was alive and well. Now if they could just manage to take her without sounding an alarm to the henchmen guarding her, who must be somewhere nearby...

The cousins came to the edge of the lighted chamber and soon realized it was a side cave that had been turned into an actual room. The old woman had her back to them as she changed the little girl's diaper. Beyond the two females was a narrow walkway that must lead out to the main cavern. That would undoubtedly be where the guards were stationed.

What to do about the grandmother? And would the child create a fuss and draw the guards?

Lucas turned to Hunter and gave a shake of his head. Placing a finger to his lips, he smiled and indicated Hunter should stay where he was.

It took only a few steps to reach the old woman. Lucas flowed like a shadow, making no sound. In a flashy move, he drew a knife with one hand and placed the palm of the other across the woman's mouth.

"I know you've wished for an escape, Grandmother," he whispered into her ear in Navajo. "We're from the Brotherhood and have come to free you."

The old lady never jerked or whimpered. She simply nodded her head to indicate she understood.

"Bring the child," Lucas said as he dropped his hand from her mouth. He turned his back to her, but continued to hold his knife, facing the doorway outside.

The woman picked up the baby in silence. She folded her into a large shawl and then fastened the ends around her neck. Next she picked up a dozen baby-related items and shoved them into her wide, deep pockets. The old grandmother was obviously a practical and savvy woman.

When she was done, she turned to face Hunter. He inched backward into the dark shaft behind him. They would have to leave the same way they'd come. But could the old lady make it carrying the baby?

Lucas turned to him and nodded, as though he'd read his thoughts again. He came toward them, crossing the chamber with silent steps.

"You lead, cousin," he told Hunter when he got close, and handed him the flashlight. "Go now."

Hunter knew better than to argue. They had a very short window of opportunity to get away.

As they moved up the slippery, slanting path in near darkness, he began a sacred chant under his breath that would help keep them safe. But whenever he let his mind wander, the fear of being apprehended before they reached daylight wriggled into his consciousness and made him falter.

On one of those slips, he heard Lucas murmur, "Concentrate on the chants. Keep moving."

With some kind of womanly magic, the old grandmother kept her balance and also kept the baby quiet. Only once did the child make so much as a gurgling sound during the climb.

The absolute worst moments, though, were when Hunter's mind turned to Bailey. Then the darkness seemed to close in on him. Had the Skinwalkers found her by now? What would happen to her?

But he let his anger at the Skinwalkers help him fight off those thoughts. He'd found a way to keep moving by imagining an end to their terrible scourge. Up he went. Climbing closer and closer to freedom and safety.

Closer to everything that now mattered the most.

Chapter 10

"Oh, thank heaven!" Bailey squealed when she saw Hunter's profile framed in the coyote cave's entrance.

Thrilled and trembling, she couldn't make her feet move at all as Hunter, Lucas and an old woman carrying Tara all ducked into the shadowy cave.

Finally.

When her mind and body got themselves in sync, Bailey propelled herself toward the weary group. But it wasn't the baby girl she ran for.

Flinging herself into Hunter's arms, she began to hyperventilate. "You're here! You've rescued the baby! You—you…" She was out of words and out of breath.

Hunter held her close. As he did, a bolt of heat flashed between them, so strong she nearly backed away. She refused to give the sudden electricity much credence, though, the same way she refused to think of all the negative possibilities that might be in their future. Instead, she snuggled closer.

"It's okay, slick." Hunter gazed into her eyes as if she were the last drop of water on earth and he was dying of thirst. "We made it back without anyone following us. Lucas says he's not sensing the Skinwalkers chasing us yet."

Hunter rubbed a thumb under her eyes to wipe away the tears. "You and Michael didn't have any trouble here, did you?" He was inspecting her as if he feared she was damaged in some hidden way.

Managing only a shake of her head, Bailey could barely think, let alone speak. She hadn't realized how full of tension and fear she'd been until the sight of him had released it all.

"The baby seems okay so far," Hunter told her softly. "The old Navajo the Skinwalkers hired is a good woman. She's taken excellent care of the child and says Tara is fine."

Bailey stood on tiptoe to look around Hunter's shoulder at the two. The woman was removing the baby from a big shawl that had been tied around her neck. The child looked terrific.

"Tara's really all right?" she asked Hunter. "The Skinwalkers didn't hurt her?"

"Go see for yourself. She's really okay. That Navajo grandmother seems more than capable of caring for her."

"Um...you're sure the old lady isn't one of *them?*"

"Positive," he declared with a wry smile. "Lucas read her thoughts when we took them from the cavern. The grandmother had apparently overheard the evil ones planning to kill both of them. And she was smart enough to realize her only hope of keeping herself and Tara alive was with the Brotherhood."

Hunter loosened his grip on Bailey's waist, stepped back and nodded toward the baby. "Go on. It's okay."

Trying to keep from dashing forward in excitement, she instead tiptoed quietly.

Tara truly looked wonderful. Well-fed and happy. The Navajo grandmother had been a great caretaker, obviously much better than Bailey and her amateur attempts.

The woman was apparently a traditionalist. Bailey recognized that from her own grandmother's lessons. Like all other well-trained Dine, the elder kept her eyes averted and did not look directly at Bailey. She said something in Navajo, and then held Tara out to her.

Hunter replied to the old lady, and then came up behind Bailey. "She asked if you are the one who saved this child during the forced trek across the desert," he whispered. "I told her you were."

"Saved? Me?" Bailey was trembling as she took Tara into her arms. "Tell her I only did what anyone would've. I'm no hero."

Tara opened her sleepy eyes and looked up at Bailey. The little girl babbled a few baby words and held her chubby arms out to the very woman who'd just claimed to be no hero.

Bailey's knees grew weak. She felt a steadying hand on her shoulder, and knew Hunter was right behind her and ready to hold her upright if necessary.

It wasn't. The warmth of his touch gave her back her old determination. Her strength returned in a rush.

"Do I have time to play with the baby for a while?" Hugging Tara to her chest, Bailey turned and carried her toward the piñon needle bed.

"Yes," Hunter told her. "We all need some rest, and should be safely hidden here for an hour or so. Then

Michael will take you and Tara and the old woman back to civilization. Lucas and I will protect your backs and create diversions in another direction if necessary."

Bailey plopped down with Tara and stared up at him. She opened her mouth to argue. There was no way she'd be leaving the desert without Hunter. He could just forget that idea.

The man was so special, so real and honest and good. And yet he didn't seem to see any of that about himself. She simply could not walk away from him, not knowing whether he would still be alive for tomorrow's sunrise.

His face became a mask of steel. He clearly expected her to throw a fit over leaving with the others, and seemed sure she would try getting her own way. So she didn't try.

She didn't say a word, but set her jaw in steel, mimicking his. And made a final decision. When the time came, she wouldn't allow him to force her to go anywhere unless he went, too. No arguments. No questions. Period.

"A map?" Hunter was shocked. Why would a map be important enough to Skinwalkers to bring about this chaos? And how could a mere map be the reason he might be destined to die? It seemed all too confusing and trivial.

The three cousins squatted on their heels in a dark corner of the coyote cave, whispering and plotting their escape. Meanwhile, the females slept quietly on the soft piñon branches around the fire pit.

Because none of their cell phones were working in these cliffs, Lucas had received a message from the Brotherhood through the help of the Bird People. A map was supposed to be the 'trade' for the child. But the Skinwalkers had managed a magician's trick and exchanged a doll in place of the real baby. The evil ones had gotten away with the map, and apparently still believed they had the baby stashed back in their cavern.

Willie Concho had lied, managing to sneak away from the FBI and the Brotherhood for the exchange without telling them. He'd hoped to save the child by secretly complying with what the Skinwalkers demanded. But he'd also had an agenda of his own—along with a secret plan to beat them at their own game.

Now, finding himself tricked and without hope, the old man was devastated. Positive his mistake in not confiding in the FBI would be the cause of his only granddaughter's death, Willie Concho was begging for help.

Hunter's brother, Kody, had talked privately with him about the map after Willie returned from the exchange. Kody then passed the information along to Lucas via the Bird People.

"Nearly six months ago Hastiin Concho found a shallow cave in a cliff overlooking the river. It'd been hidden by water for centuries." Lucas repeated the story he'd been told by the birds. "When the drought first uncovered the cave, Willie crawled inside and found a half-buried stone container. It held an animal skin with marks resembling a map. On it he saw a drawing of a river and one of a monolith, both done in pictograph style. But that's about all he remembers.

"He hid the map in his safe right away," Lucas continued, "knowing the thing must be ancient and priceless. He figured to sell it to some museum, making another fortune to go along with the one he made selling off coal leases."

Michael narrowed his eyes. "Did Concho copy any of the markings down? Did he take photos or drawings of it before he turned the map over to the Skinwalkers?"

Lucas solemnly shook his head. "He thought he was too smart to lose control of something so priceless to a crazy Skinwalker witch. And he certainly didn't want any evidence of what he'd discovered left behind for the FBI to find.

"Willie was absolutely positive he would be able to trick the Skinwalkers and end up with both the map and the baby. He now knows better."

"This new Navajo Wolf and his soldiers are clever." Michael looked thoughtful for a moment. "How did the Skinwalkers learn of the existence of the map?"

Lucas shrugged. "That was not in the Bird People's message. But I gather it must've been from a spy who either worked for or was friends with Willie."

Hunter broke into the discussion. "It doesn't matter. The map is gone. We need to plan how best to get the child and the women out of here."

Michael put a hand on his cousin's arm. "That map might be crucial in turning the tide of this war in the Skinwalker's favor. There must be a good reason why it's worth so much to them. I'll need to review the Skinwalker legends when we return."

"You do that, cousin," Hunter said, with far too much sarcasm for a Navajo. "In the meantime, how the hell are we going to get the women back to their families without all of us being killed?"

Lucas and Michael exchanged quiet looks. Hunter knew he'd sounded out of balance and annoyed. Too bad. He would never find his way back to harmony until Bailey was safe with her father. And he was smart enough to know she would never agree to going without the baby. They had been down that road a few times before.

"We gave a plan some discussion while you slept,"

Lucas said. "Five of us trekking through the desert or over the cliffs would be too obvious. Rather like waving a red flag at the Skinwalkers to come get us."

"But I understood Michael had an SUV parked nearby," Hunter stated. "Can't we all sneak there during the night? If we're lucky, we can be miles away before the Skinwalkers notice a thing."

Michael was shaking his head. "It's too dangerous. In the first place, my SUV is parked upwind from that missionary's cabin near the well, where the Skinwalkers first took the child. We drove out here on the old wagon trail. But we stopped short, about a mile away, when we hit the wide-open desert surrounding the cabin. Going back to the SUV the fastest way would leave our larger group far too exposed."

Hunter nodded.

"And in the second place," Michael continued, "all of us going the same direction at the same time is not a sound security action. We need a point man and someone who follows. And for a plan to make any sense in this situation, we would need a good diversionary tactic."

Hunter could hear the hesitant note in Michael's voice. And he didn't at all like what he figured was coming. He raised his chin, eyed his cousins and waited.

"Our understanding is that the Skinwalker Dog believes you and Bailey are dead," Lucas stated. "Killed by fire and smoke in that shaft in the cliffs. I'm sensing that he believes the Brotherhood has sent a different tracker here to steal the grandmother and the baby back."

Leaning back on his heels, Hunter waited to hear the plan. But he was already unhappy with his cousins' hedging.

"We need some way of sending the Skinwalkers off in

the wrong direction while we slip the baby and the grand-mother away. A couple of us can sneak them out through the open desert to the SUV."

"All three females," Hunter corrected. But through the darkness he saw Lucas's deep ebony eyes watching him closely.

"We have to think clearly here, cousin," Lucas said softly. "Not with our sentiment. The wrong move could cost everyone's life."

Lucas spoke quietly but firmly. "Getting rid of the grandmother is the evil ones' main concern. They will be after her, but they won't care a lot about finding the grand-mother…and Bailey is already cut from their thoughts."

"Hold it," Hunter exclaimed. "If you're about to suggest that we use Bailey as some kind of a decoy, don't bother. It won't happen."

Hearing a sudden rustling behind him, he turned his head to find her on her hands and knees, crawling toward them.

"Did I hear my name?" she asked when she got close enough to whisper.

"Go back to sleep," Hunter snapped. "Watch after the child."

She screwed up her mouth and sat down with the men. "The grandmother is changing Tara. She does a much better job of watching the baby than I ever could. I want to help with the escape plans."

"No—" he started to argue.

"Good idea," Michael and Lucas chimed together.

"Explain it to me, please," she asked Hunter's cousins. But she kept her eyes trained on him as she spoke the words, daring him to fight with the lot of them.

Hunter sat back and folded his arms over his chest.

"The Skinwalkers believe you and Hunter are already dead," Michael told her. "And the caretaker grandmother claims she overheard them talking about killing her and the child so there would be no witnesses."

"They'll be looking for those two, but not for me. Is that what you think?"

Michael nodded. "In fact, we believe they might ignore you altogether, even if they manage to catch you. You and Hunter seem to be totally unimportant to them now."

"Okay. The grandmother is the one in the most danger, and probably Tara, too. I've got that. What can I do to make them safe?"

Michael answered, "Help us create a diversion. We need time—or maybe just a little confusion. Either should do the trick."

"No." Hunter sat straight up. "I won't allow it. All the females must go back together."

"*You* won't allow it?" Bailey had to grind her teeth together to keep from telling him off in front of his cousins. She tugged on his shirtsleeve and pulled him around so she could whisper to him without the others hearing everything she said.

"Uh…" She hesitated as he narrowed his gaze to a cold stare. But it was up to her to be strong. "Look. I appreciate all you've done for me. Really. But you have no right to tell me what I can or can't do. We've already had this discussion once before, and just look how far we've come from then.

"Tara is almost safe," she continued. "The baby's out of Skinwalker hands. With a few more hours and the right plan, she'll be with her mother. I have to help make that happen."

He looked so angry—and isolated. It hurt her to see those emotions in the man she loved.

Bailey wasn't trying to make him mad or to hurt him.

She wasn't even trying to make him say he loved her and wanted to keep her safe. She was *so* over that. Understanding, finally, that they would never have a permanent relationship, she'd already decided to move on.

She loved Hunter, maybe more than she would ever love anyone else in her entire life. But she couldn't allow him to rule her actions. Not when she'd finally discovered what was really worth living for. And not when he would be long gone as soon as they were back to civilization.

"Hunter, please listen," she begged. "You have given me the most wonderful of presents. I know now what I'm capable of doing. Thank you for that. But if you make me stop without finishing what I started, it will destroy my confidence and probably send me right back to the drugs.

"If you care anything about me—" Bailey broke off abruptly, immediately wishing she could take back those words.

What if he'd decided he *didn't* care? Or if all he wanted now was to return her to her father. Maybe the only thing he really wanted was for them to share another roll in the hay, and he didn't give a rip about what any of it might cost her.

Too late to quit talking. She had to continue. "Please don't stop me this time. I beg you. I'll do whatever else you ask. Give you anything you want. Anything."

The sudden hurt look in his eyes was nearly her undoing. She'd said too much. Gone too far. A sob bubbled up her throat, but she forced a cough to keep it contained.

Hunter coldly turned his back and spoke to his cousins. "Tell us your plan."

While dusk created additional shadows on the sand-stone monoliths and orange-colored buttes, Bailey tried to stay behind Hunter. He was moving fast, in a zigzag pattern, back through the desert and cliffs on nearly the same path that the Skinwalkers had taken with her and the baby.

She couldn't seem to stop her stupid sniffling. She'd won. But in winning, she'd lost him for good.

The only positive result that could come from her hateful words would be having Tara safely back in her mother's arms. Michael and Lucas had spirited the baby and the old woman away just before dawn, with a quick dash across the desert. They'd headed straight for the SUV Michael had hidden a few miles away, and hopefully they'd made it out to the main highway by now.

Bailey was wearing the old woman's shawl. She kept her head and neck bent in the way of an old Navajo grandmother, creating a diversion. A couple of full canteens lay inside the shawl, making it look as though Bailey was carrying Tara.

The plan was for her and Hunter to build a fire, make a lot of noise and then start crossing the mesa. Lucas hadn't sensed anyone looking for them yet, but if the Skinwalkers showed up too soon, she and Hunter would be leading them in the opposite direction from the baby.

If anything went wrong with their scheme and they didn't make it back to Hunter's SUV before the Skinwalkers caught up, the Bird People were going to bring reinforcements.

It sounded like a good enough plan to Bailey. But Hunter hadn't spoken one word since they'd started out.

One slim ray of hope that he wouldn't hate her forever came when he'd insisted he would be the one to travel with her. The two of them were to be decoys. Michael and Lucas shared the responsibility of getting Tara back to her family safe and sound.

Still, tears kept on leaking from Bailey's eyes and rolling down her cheeks. Hunter's face had been so full of hurt when she'd gotten her own way, despite his wishes. She was trying not to think about his pain, but there didn't seem to be any hope of forgetting it long enough to slow down the tears.

"Hold it." Hunter reached out and grabbed her by the arm. "You seem to have a real suicidal instinct these days, slick. But I'm not willing to be the one left explaining your demise to your father."

"Suicidal? What?" She stopped moving and looked up at him for an explanation.

He nodded to a spot directly in front of her. "We are not out for a morning jog, Ms. Howard. Watch your step."

She still didn't see what was the big deal. But moving to her left around a purple sagebrush, she found the edge of a narrow arroyo suddenly right in front of her. Another two feet and she would've fallen down a fifty-foot drop.

"Oh." Her knees buckled, and she sat down hard in the sand. "Wow. I…" Her dry throat made speech impossible.

Hunter crouched beside her and held out his canteen. "Take a few sips of water."

Trying to lift her hands to grab the container, Bailey discovered she was as limp as overcooked spaghetti. She raised her eyes to meet his, and silently pleaded with him for assistance.

As mean and demanding as she'd been earlier, he should've ignored her. But he didn't. That would not have been Hunter's style.

"Here. Let me help." He slid his arm around her shoulders so he could get closer. Gently lifting the canteen to her lips, he helped her take a drink.

Instantly those old devil tears were back, welling in her

eyes. This time even worse than before. How could he be so damn kind?

She sniffed and bit her cheek, trying to restrain the sob threatening to bubble out of her mouth.

He patted her shoulder. "You're okay. I won't let any hidden catastrophes do you in. At least not until I get you back to your father. And then I may kill you myself."

That did it. The floodgates opened and tears streamed down her cheeks. Huge, gasping sobs poured forth. Her nose started to run, and no doubt turned bright red, the way it did when she was stone drunk.

She didn't want him to be nice. Why couldn't he get mad and yell at her, for God's sake? Or go far, far away...

But he didn't move. He stayed right beside her, turned her into his chest and let her cry it out.

After a few minutes, she stemmed the shakes that had been racking her body. Leaning her head back, she looked up at his face through watery eyes. His jaw was set.

She was tired. She must be, because the impulse to kiss him was strong. That would be so wrong at this point.

From high above their heads, a sudden loud, shrieking noise filled the air. "What's that?" she asked.

"Hell," Hunter spat as he lifted her into his arms. "We've stayed in one place too long. The Skinwalkers must be close behind us."

Chapter 11

He'd made a couple of mistakes. And they might have cost them their lives.

Hunter had been heading toward a winter hogan, one belonging to his mother's clan. His family members were still up in the mountains for the summer with the sheep. Their empty place would've been a good spot to hide for the night.

He'd gotten close to the safety it could provide. Just not close enough.

Shifting Bailey in his arms, he moved as fast as he could. He was running among rocks and snakeweed, heading away from the rim of the slot canyon where they'd stopped. Because of her baby-disguise bundle, Bailey's body was too unwieldy to throw over his shoulder. This time he had to cradle her close to his chest like an infant.

Good thing the sun was setting. Dusk was adding its growing shadows to the boulder-strewn desert. Conditions would've been much more dangerous for them if the sun was still high in the sky, illuminating their every move.

Damn it. He simply had not counted on the extra time Bailey would need. With the added weight around her neck, she'd slowed them down. He also should've paid closer attention to where she was going. But no, not him. Instead, he'd jumped out in front.

He'd known she was keeping her eyes lowered in the manner of the grandmother. What had he been thinking to allow her to wander around like that behind his back? There were far too many dangers in the desert.

"Are they gaining on us?" Her muffled question came as a shock. He'd almost forgotten she wasn't a dead weight he'd been toting in his arms.

He shook his head. "No time to find out." It was the most he could tell her. The most his fear and lung capacity would allow.

Even if he'd known for sure the Skinwalkers were right behind them, he wasn't positive he would've told her. Not if there was still a chance he could save her life.

The thought of dying made his legs pump faster, propelling him closer to the base of a series of buttes leading to the escarpment known as White Rock Bench. Right beyond there, in a surprising wildflower-filled valley, was his clan's winter hogan.

As they entered the deep shade of a familiar sheep trail, Hunter took his first solid breath since hearing the Bird People's warning. This spot was less than a five minute run from the hogan. He might actually make it there before the Skinwalkers caught up to them.

He kept his mouth firmly shut and plowed on.

A few minutes later, he crashed through his great-aunt's

garden fence and rounded the west side of the hogan. When he came to the doorway on the eastern side, he skidded to a halt and set Bailey on her feet.

Grabbing the padlock key out of its rock hiding place, he opened the lock, then kicked open the door. "Inside. Hurry."

"Whose place…?"

"Go!" He gave her a little shove and pushed her across the threshold. It was all he could do to keep from grabbing her up bodily and shot-putting her into the room. Thirty seconds later he'd shut and barricaded the door behind them. "Get rid of the disguise."

"What?"

"Take off that shawl and the scarf on your head. Now." He went back out for a second to switch on the generators.

When he returned, sparks of energy were bouncing off her like static electricity. He could almost see them lighting up the dark room.

Turning his back, he moved around the main living quarters of the hogan, flipping on a few lights and pulling window coverings shut. The hogan had been partially modernized over the years. Real glass windows, electricity to power lights and even a few basic kitchen appliances had been installed. A small modern bathroom had been added last year.

When he came around the bathroom door, he found Bailey standing exactly where he'd left her. "You still determined to commit suicide on this trek, slick?"

"Why are you being rude?" she snapped. "Are you so furious with me that you're willing to ruin the plan?"

"Huh?" What the hell was she talking about? "One."

He held up his forefinger and scowled. "If you don't get out of that getup before the Skinwalkers show up, you'll be dead before you can explain you are not the one they're looking for. *Two*, the *plan* called for us to lead them away from the others, not to be attacked before we can get out of here. *Three*, if you think I've been rude so far, just keep stãnding there staring at me." He took a step toward her, and she ripped off the shawl and scarf before he could take another one.

He opened a storage locker and found some women's clothes.

"Here." He threw them in her general direction. "Put these on and be quick about it. You're going to invite them in when they show up and you're going to act like you belong here. Maybe then we'll live long enough to see the end of this terrific plan."

She turned her back and pulled the long maroon skirt over the rags of her ruined suit. That she'd thought to turn away from his gaze almost made him smile.

"Hurry up. Put that blouse on, too. When they make a noise outside, indicating they expect to be invited in like any Dine visitor, you will step out the door and wave at them."

"I'm supposed to invite the Skinwalkers inside to kill us?"

Hunter had to suck in a deep breath to keep from raising his voice. "Remember what Lucas said? The Skinwalkers don't care about us. They think we're dead. It's the baby and the grandmother they want. They won't come to the door in their animal personas. And there won't be any grandmother and baby here for them to find, just a young Navajo couple. If we answer their questions and don't stand in their way, they should just leave us alone."

She rubbed her arms as though she was cold. "I don't much care for that word *should*. What if these aren't Skinwalkers, but the same two goons who kidnapped me and Tara?"

Ignoring her for the moment, he stepped outside the door and flipped the switch for the electric lights that had been recently installed on tall poles at the edge of the yard. Next he searched the big front room for a hiding place for the rifle and pack that no ordinary shepherd would have. The only possibility was in the storage locker with the clothes. He shoved both items under towels and underwear. Finally, he pulled a gimmee cap off a hook beside the door and fitted it over his hair. The two of them had to appear the same as any sheep-camp Navajos.

"Those two goons never got a good look at me," he finally answered. "Remember to keep your eyes lowered. Stare right at them and we're both dead. Don't say too much, either. Stick to yes and no. Your Navajo is not the greatest."

He heard her puff out a breath. She was still furious. Good. Anger might keep her alive, and it was definitely easier on him than all those tears had been.

Both of them stood stock-still and stared at the closed door. The normal evening winds had picked up and a warm southwesterly breeze blew around the eight-sided hogan, soft as a mother's breath against her child's cheek. There were no noises at all that sounded like Skinwalkers.

Five minutes later the two of them were still standing there, staring at the door and listening. Hunter didn't know for sure about Bailey, but the waiting was killing him.

"What if that wasn't Skinwalkers behind us in the desert?" she whispered after another minute. "What if they're not coming? What if—"

A shrill whistle pierced the air, cutting through her next whispered question. Hunter felt his gut twist.

Bailey spun toward the door and reached for the handle.

"Hold on, slick." He walked closer and put a steadying hand on her shoulder. "Give them a minute or two. We don't want it to look like we were standing around waiting for them."

She screwed up her mouth and scowled at him. "Not funny," she whispered.

But she did wait another full minute before she pulled open the door and walked outside. Hunter crept over to the window next to the door and drew aside the curtain so he could see the front yard. If anything went wrong with this little meeting, all he had to defend them was the knife stuffed in his boot.

He saw three figures in the distance. Each of the men was using his human form, but they were too far away for him to get a decent look. Bailey raised a hand and waved.

"Good. Now lower your eyes and come back inside." He was whispering to her as loudly as he dared through the half-closed door.

When she was back in the big room with the door closed behind her, he quickly gave her last-minute instructions. "Let me do the talking. Stand in the shadows. Don't raise your face and don't look at them."

She narrowed her eyes and her lips flattened into tight thin strips. But she turned and moved back into the darkness of the next alcove.

Hunter opened the door again to find two men standing at the threshold. He didn't want to appear too curious, but he couldn't understand why only two of the three had come to the door.

"Ya'at'eeh." Trying to keep his eyes averted, he stepped aside and indicated the men could enter.

"Ya'at'eeh." The first one, a man he didn't recognize, repeated the standard greeting as he moved into the room.

The second man was right behind him, and Hunter nearly jumped out of his skin. He was one of the goons who had kidnapped Bailey and the baby. It would be a cold day in an Anglo hell before Hunter ever forgot the face he'd seen in his binoculars.

These weren't the Skinwalkers, but merely hired hands again. It wouldn't do Hunter a bit of good to begin one of the ancient chants to fight them off.

Worse yet, would this smelly idiot recognize Bailey?

The first man who'd entered did the talking. He asked about a grandmother and a child. Hunter kept his eyes down and told him no such females had been to the hogan recently, and that the rest of their clan remained in the mountains.

That same guy moved toward Bailey and asked if she had a child here. She kept her eyes lowered and denied it with a single quiet word.

Hunter held his breath, waiting for the second man to recognize her. But he never moved from his spot right inside the door. His eyes traveled over every surface in the place, but he never acknowledged Bailey.

It seemed like hours, but after a couple of tense minutes, the two men turned and walked out. Hunter stepped across the threshold and watched them leave. As they moved under one of the yard lights, the third man rejoined them and Hunter got a good look at his profile.

At that one surprising sight, Hunter sucked in a lungful of air. Crap. It was Director Levi George, known as "Sarge" to his men at the Navajo Tribal Department of Public Safety. He was the politician who'd been appointed to head up the entire nation's tribal police department, and ultimately he was Hunter's boss.

Pulling his cap down even farther on his forehead,

Hunter quickly stepped back inside and closed the door. Of course. It had to have been Levi George's voice he'd heard right before the fire that had almost killed them in the shaft.

Levi George must be the Skinwalker Dog. Had he seen Hunter's face? Did he know he'd been spotted?

Hunter waited, listening for any sign.

"Are they gone?" Bailey went to the window and tried to peek out.

"Shush," he said as he grabbed her up and held her close. "Say nothing. Don't move."

After a few minutes of tense silence, Hunter released her and went around the cabin, turning off lights. Once they were in darkness, he went back to the window and lifted the curtain. All three men had left the yard.

"I think they're gone." He didn't intend to tell Bailey about the Skinwalker Dog or about the fact that they may have been compromised.

If Levi George knew he'd been seen, the attack would come swiftly. Hunter tried to keep panic from overtaking his good sense.

"That guy," Bailey whispered in a high-pitched tone. "The second one by the door. That was Jacquez, the smelly kidnapper. Did you see him? Do you think he recognized me?"

Hunter could hear the panic in her voice and deliberately calmed himself. "I don't think so. He never made a move for you. Probably he didn't get a good look at your face."

"What are we going to do? Where can we go?"

"Sit and be quiet," he commanded. "I have to think."

He heard her gasp and figured she must be mad at him again. It couldn't be helped. His brain had been paralyzed with fear at the sight of Levi George. Then his adrenaline had spiked, making him furious at the Navajo witches. Now he had to clear his head and figure out his and Bailey's next move.

Should they run? If so, where could they go that would offer more protection?

After his heart stopped pounding quite so loudly in his ears, Hunter remembered that this hogan had been blessed by a hataalii when it was built, and again last year, before a marriage. That may have been why the Skinwalker, Levi George, had hesitated to approach.

Hunter knew the hired goons would be fairly easy to defend against. He still had his rifle and ammunition. Why couldn't he also perform a special ceremony to help defend the entire hogan against the Skinwalkers? Then he and Bailey would be relatively safe here until morning.

His SUV was parked about ten miles away. In daylight, they could get back there in a few hours. At the same time, the Bird People could go for help and watch over them.

Yes, that was the best plan. Now all he had to do was spend the night here with Bailey, without letting his anger at the Skinwalkers keep him from doing things the right way.

Every time Hunter looked at her, his needs and wants became clear, crowding out everything else in his mind. He'd come close to losing her forever. It was terrifying. It was also arousing.

But that couldn't be. Taking a deep breath, he made a vow. He might or might not be able to control the Skinwalkers, but he could control his private thoughts.

"Why don't you eat something, slick?"

It had been hours since those men had come to the hogan. Everything was quiet. Too damn quiet, in Bailey's opinion.

"I'm not hungry."

She'd believed Hunter when he said they would be better off staying put, and that he could give the hogan a special blessing. Still, sitting here in near darkness and listening to the winds had been like waiting for the bell to ring, signaling school was out. She was going insane.

"You must eat."

"Don't tell me what to do. I'm not listening to you anymore. If we'd left here when I wanted to, I'd be back with my family by now."

"Good thinking. More likely you'd be dead. And I have no intention of dying beside you, as a result of some great plan of yours."

She heard the subdued anger as his smooth voice slid over her. Well, too frigging bad. She'd made the mistake of hurting his feelings back in front of his cousins—so what? It was time for him to let it go and start thinking about her feelings for a change.

Clinging to his anger was so typical of Hunter. She wouldn't stand for it ever again.

"I think it's safe again. I'm going to step outside for some fresh air," she said with her chin raised. "Do whatever you want, but keep your hurt feelings to yourself. There's hours and hours left until daybreak, and I'm not letting you continue to run over me the whole time."

She turned and marched toward the front door. But she hadn't taken two steps before Hunter had her by the arm and was swinging her around to face him.

"Don't be an idiot. I told you we can't go out until daylight."

"I said I'm not listening to you anymore." She covered her ears with her hands and tugged against his grip.

"That does it." He grabbed her around the waist and dragged her to him. "I've never even come close to laying a hand on a woman in anger before. But we're either going to make love right now, or I may give it a try."

Suddenly, every bit of fear and irritation disappeared. She smiled at him and batted her lashes. "I pick making love. And isn't it a coincidence? Right now my schedule appears to be free."

He muttered a Navajo curse, then crushed her mouth beneath his. It was a rare, vintage kiss. Better than any fine wine. She could feel the desperation behind it, and let anticipation fuel her movements.

She kissed him back and dug her nails into his wide, muscular shoulders. Sex with Hunter was like having dessert before dinner—fabulous and sinful. But done too often, it could ruin your self-esteem.

Just now, though, she was in the mood for being bad. Dancing on a knife's edge did that to people, she'd heard.

Moaning, Bailey urged him to hurry. He kept on kissing her as he bunched up her long skirt in one hand and cupped her bottom with the other. None of the tattered clothes she had on underneath could've stood up to the force of their desire.

Within seconds, his zipper was lowered and he'd clasped the back of her thighs. Lifting her off her feet, he backed her up to the solid bathroom door and pinned her there. She wrapped her legs around his waist while he drove himself inside her eager body with one frantic shove.

Hanging on, she met each of his wild, raw moves with her own. She lost herself in his kisses and the grinding, untamed thrusts that threatened to take her to a different place. A place far beyond flesh and base desires. A new place, full of earth, fiery fierce movements and gentle careful touching.

This was more… More emotion and more combustion. This was love.

The knowledge had been with her for days. As he drove ever deeper and bent nearly in two to suck one of her nipples into his mouth, she abandoned any pretense that making love with him could ever be just for sex.

As rough and primitive as their lovemaking was, he still took extra care to be sure she was okay. She could feel him straining to hold back for her, at least until stars exploded behind her eyelids and she quit feeling anything at all but exquisite shocks of pure pleasure.

He slammed into her one last time and then both of them stopped breathing.

Next thing she knew, he was easing her down the wall, lowering her to the ground. He ripped his shirt up over his head, while she stepped out of the skirt and lost the blouse.

They were both breathing heavily and soaked with sweat. He tipped his head toward the bathroom. "You first? The generator doesn't produce much hot water, though. So try to be quick."

She was dying to see that wonderful grin of his again. He'd looked sober and serious for days now. So she turned her back and winked at him over her shoulder. "I think I might need some help. With washing my back or with…"

His whole face lit up and that awe-inspiring, girl-trapping grin came back in a flash. He didn't wait for her to finish, but dragged her into his arms and jerked open the bathroom door.

The shower stall was tiny, but big enough for two if they stayed close. Which was fine by Bailey.

Despite their hot and heavy lovemaking, Hunter still felt the need to consume her. His blood heated faster than the water. He positioned them both under the spray, then took his time soaping her body. As he worked the slippery bar into every crevice he could find, he watched her face. At first she giggled, then her eyes glazed over and she began breathing hard.

"We're going to run out of hot water," he said at last. "Come here." He pulled her close so that the lather worked its way onto his chest.

She closed her eyes and hummed, low and sweet and full of need. Her nipples peaked and grew darker as she brushed them across his skin. The water turned lukewarm, so he hurriedly splashed them both to get rid of the soap.

While the spray grew colder, her skin got hotter. Hot and smooth and wet. And more delectable than a poor guy like him could possibly stand.

Liquid fire was racing over his own skin, replacing the soap lather. He turned off the shower and backed her against the tile.

He wanted to taste everything. He'd never been a greedy man; that way led to being out of harmony. But just now, he was desperate to have it all.

Rubbing his hands over her dripping body, he dragged his mouth and teeth along her jawline, then down her neck. Her head fell back, and her moan echoed off the shower walls.

He nipped each extended tip as he licked a path down between her breasts, and then circled her navel with his tongue. Kneeling before her, he gripped her bottom to hold her still, and nuzzled her belly.

Bailey's thighs were quivering and there was an earthquake in her knees. She wasn't sure she could continue to stand.

Then she felt Hunter's warm breath in her most tender

of places. The blood pounded in her ears as his moist mouth and tongue danced into hidden spots, igniting her.

Lost again, she reached out for the man she loved.

Chapter 12

Bailey drove her hands into his hair and held his head. It was all she could do to keep herself steady as he continued exploring her body with his mouth and tongue. Hearing a scream, she was amazed to find it had come from her own throat.

She pleaded with him to hurry. But Hunter was relentless. He drew her up with his mouth, then slowed his movements, leaving her hovering frantically on the edge. Minutes went by while she cried his name and begged for release.

Finally, when she was cursing him and promising to permanently damage his anatomy, she at last felt the beginnings of an all-consuming shudder roll wildly through her body. She must've forgotten to breathe. As she sagged against him, her internal muscles convulsed again and again—and she totally blacked out.

When she opened her eyes, they were lying side by side

on top of a thick pile of Navajo blankets on the floor of the main room. She turned and smiled at him.

"You okay?" he murmured.

She nodded and rolled closer. "Better than okay."

They made love again. This time with a tenderness that nearly brought back the tears.

Over and over they reached for each other through the darkest hours of the night. With soft sighs and pleasured gasps, they explored one another's bodies and experimented with erotic techniques.

Bailey rediscovered what she'd learned as a girl—that Hunter was a strong man who knew how and when to be vulnerable. She also came to an important revelation somewhere in the middle of having him pin her arms above her head while her legs draped over his shoulders. This was a night to end all nights. A night and a love to remember.

Something was tickling his nose. Hunter opened his eyes and found himself curled around a sleeping Bailey, with his face buried in her hair.

Not ready to disturb her yet, he inched closer to her naked body, then lay quietly, watching her sleep. Thinking about their fantastic night and about how he would like to have many, many more of them, he felt his gut wrench in response.

A long-term relationship with her would be impossible. She had been raised in the city and belonged there. He had been raised in Dinetah and belonged here.

Maybe he could find a way to exist in her rich and fast world. Maybe. But it would have to be after the Brotherhood brought an end to the Skinwalkers' reign of terror. And then it would have to wait until after he finished his contracted service with the Tribal Police. And then…

No, it was even more than all that.

She was the sun. Brilliant. Out there. Shining her light for everyone to see.

And he was the moon. Quiet. Smiling. Only showing part of the whole at any one time.

They didn't mesh. They never would.

Bailey stirred, turned on her back and then yawned. "Hey." She rolled over to face him.

"Hey, yourself."

She reached out for him, the same way she had throughout the night. But it was nearly dawn, so he took her hands in his own and held her still.

"We need to move. Pack up, eat something then leave. Let's not make any mistakes at the last moment."

"Okay." She'd said the word tentatively, as though she was well aware that their sensual time together was coming to an abrupt halt. That they would never be together this way again.

Rolling on her side and sitting up, she ran a hand through her hair. "Yuck. Mind if I get in the bathroom first?"

"Not if you don't take very long."

"Don't worry. I won't. How long will it take you to fix us something to eat? I'm starved."

He'd been turning over to sit up when she'd made that pronouncement and nearly crashed into the table leg beside their blanket. She was hungry? Before she'd said food was the last thing she wanted in the morning.

Something had really changed. But he wasn't about to say anything. Not him. He'd rather live through the day, thanks.

True to her word, Bailey was back out of the bathroom in less than ten minutes. Amazing.

He'd found some of his great-aunt's canned mutton

stew and had heated it on the cookstove, which stood in the middle of the room, as in all traditional hogans. He'd also found a sealed tin of cornmeal and made fry bread to go with the stew. Maybe that didn't qualify as breakfast food where Bailey came from, but it would have to do.

"Mmm. Great. I didn't know you could cook." She was working on her second bowl of stew.

"Sure. When I was a kid helping my mother's clan with their sheep, I learned to make a few things over a campfire. Shepherds usually stay overnight on the hillsides or in the fields to protect their animals from predators."

"That must've been an interesting part of your childhood. Better, at least, than the time you spent with your father, I would imagine."

He nodded and then stuffed the last bite of stew into his mouth.

"I meant to ask this when we talked about your father before…. What was your mother doing while you and your dad were out driving around Navajoland?"

Swallowing with difficulty, Hunter tried to answer the question. "My mother was a schoolteacher. She home-schooled me, and worked part-time with others when I was away."

"How come she didn't do that with your brother?"

"Kody went to boarding school. That's the traditional thing for Navajo kids to do. At one time, the federal government insisted on boarding schools for reservation kids. Some of those schools exist even today in Dinetah.

"Back when Kody was small," he explained, "my mother was still hoping that if she kept everything according to tradition, the way she'd been taught, my father would see us in balance and find some harmony of his own."

Hunter stood and poured himself a cup of the boiled coffee he'd made out of old saved grounds. "But it never happened. She gave up by the time I was old enough to attend school."

"You told me your dad did move the family back to Dinetah, right? And he *was* learning the language and the traditions from you. He must've been trying."

Shaking his head, Hunter took a sip of the sludge in his cup. "That wasn't an attempt to find harmony. I'm not sure why learning the traditions seemed so important to my father. But it probably had something to do with money. That man was one of the greediest people I've ever known. All he cared about was money and women."

"That's just awful. What did your mother have to say about the women? Why didn't she leave him?"

Hunter set his cup down, hesitating to tell her. Should he spit it out? He'd never told anyone in his whole life. Not even his own brother. Was it time to finally say it? And could he trust Bailey with the truth?

Yes, with a moment's reflection, he knew he trusted her with everything. Besides that, after today he no doubt would stop seeing much of the wealthy Ms. Howard. And she would probably forget all about her affair with the Navajo policeman.

Taking a breath, he began, "My father abused my mother. Beat her. Even broke her bones sometimes. He threatened to kill her and Kody, and me, too, if she ever told anyone or tried to leave him."

Bailey put a hand over her mouth to conceal a gasp. It was a bad image, he knew. But it was one he lived with every day of his life.

"Did you see him do it?" she asked with a frown. "Hit her?"

"Sure. Oh, my old man mostly waited until I was in bed before he let her have it. But occasionally his temper got the better of him when I was still in the room."

"Did he hit you, too?"

"Just the one time I tried to interfere. He clipped me good in the chest. Knocked the wind out of me. That was when I was ten. The jerk didn't live long enough for me to grow up and take him on. And he was too much of a coward to touch her when my older brother was home. Kody was big enough by then to make him sorry he ever had a temper."

"So Kody didn't try to stop him, either?"

"Kody didn't know. The beatings only started after he'd gone. No one knew. I really believed my father when he said he would kill all of us if my mother or I told anyone. I already told you he was a killer. He wouldn't have blinked an eye over our dead bodies."

Hell. That whole miserable story sounded both trite and perverse, even to his own ears. Hunter was truly sorry he'd said anything.

Now Bailey would think the worst of him. Think, as he did, that he would end up being exactly like his father.

Hunter figured it was time to change the subject.

"My mother has never agreed to tell Kody any of this. She claims it would only hurt him, and there's nothing anyone can do now. But, hopefully, she is finally finding some happiness," he said with a smile. "She's getting married again. This time, the guy had better be good to her…or else. I'm no kid anymore."

He didn't want to tell Bailey that he and his mother had never been able to talk through what had happened to them. Or that he had been too sick to his stomach when she'd broken a bone in a car accident to even visit her. Broken bones and his mother were much too familiar and too horrifying to bear.

All that made him sound like a coward. So he kept his mouth shut.

Instead, he grinned like he always did to cover his troubles, and started picking up their dirty plates.

"Hunter?"

"Yeah?" His hands were full of dishes, but he stopped and turned to look at her.

"I love you."

The dishes hit the floor and made a terrible clattering noise. Where the hell had that come from?

"Uh…"

"Oh, you don't have to love me in return. It's okay. I'm not a kid anymore, either. I've been to rehab and have spent hours and hours with a psychiatrist. I'm fully aware, at long last, that not everything you want wants you back."

"Uh…" He couldn't think, the adrenaline was rushing through his veins again. "Damn it, slick…I mean, Bailey. This is really not a good time to talk about such things. Your life is in danger." He would try to be reasonable, even if his brain had actually flown up the chimney pipe the minute she'd spoken the words. "We've been out in the desert, away from your family and friends, for nearly a week. You're still in shock from being kidnapped and nearly burned alive. You can't know—"

"I love you, Hunter. Maybe I have since the moment we met eight years ago. Circumstances don't change that. I've tried to change it, but I couldn't. *You* can't even change it. Though I know you've tried, too. That's just the way it is." She gave him a weak smile and shrugged. "I thought I should actually tell you—in case I don't make it back."

Hearing her talk about her own death brought him sharply into reality. He sat down next to her and picked up her hand.

"Thank you," he whispered. "Thank you for trying to make me feel like I'm decent. Like I'm not a clone of my father. No one has ever cared enough about me to take the trouble. But, Bailey, you are not about to die. We will get out of this. In a few more hours you'll be back home to civilization. Back in your family's arms. Back to long hot showers and shoe shopping. I swear it."

She was shaking her head. "You think I'm only trying to make you feel good? Don't be an ass. People can change their lives," she insisted. "I can. I know it. None of us is born with *bad* genes. Beating your wife is not hereditary. Neither is being terminally self-absorbed, like I was."

Now she had *him* shaking his head. But she wouldn't let him get a word in before she forged ahead.

"You are a good man. Look what you're doing with your life. You fight crime during the day as a cop. And at night you're secretly fighting the Skinwalkers in order to save the world. You've become a medicine man to help your clan. You care about your mother's welfare and you love your brother. What more can you do to prove it to yourself? You are not now, never were and never will be like your father."

"*You've* changed, I agree," he interjected as she took a breath. "Anyone can see that. You've beaten your addiction, and now you've discovered how strong you really can be. You're amazing. But I am not in your league, slick. Not even close. When you're home, back having lunch with your friends, you won't even notice I'm not around. I'll just be that guy who helped you save the baby from a crazy group of witches."

He dropped her hand and stood. "It's time to clear out. The sun's up. We have to go."

Bailey opened her mouth to say something else. The man was still the most frustrating son of a gun she had ever encountered. She wasn't about to go back to her old friends and her old ways. Not now. She'd changed forever.

Arguing with him would be useless, however. So she shut her mouth and shoved her chair back to help clean up.

She used a broom for the first time in her life. Sweeping up the remnants of broken dishes was probably easier than washing them would've been.

As Hunter washed the frying pan and tidied up the bathroom, her brain was working overtime. Somehow in all his denial, in all that long story about his family, she could swear he was trying to tell her he was in love with her, too.

Was it just her imagination? Did she want it so badly she believed it must be true?

He acted like a man who was afraid. Not of being exactly like his father; Bailey was positive any man she loved couldn't be that dumb.

But Hunter certainly seemed afraid to give in to his love, for some reason she couldn't quite grasp yet.

She would understand it all eventually. If the two of them really did live through the coming day, figuring out Hunter was going to become her newest project.

Desperately in love with him now, Bailey knew she always would be. She'd said it out loud, and she felt it in every fiber and cell of her body.

Maybe she was destined to become the oldest Navajo groupie on earth. She'd be following Hunter around, while he fought crime and flirted with all the girls, until they were both stooped and gray.

Hmm. Or maybe not. That wasn't such a great picture. But she was still determined to stick with him until she understood where he was coming from.

"You ready to take those last few miles back home, slick?"

He was standing in the doorway, waiting for her to walk out ahead of him. Seeing him with the sunlight catching in his hair, her heart flipped over and lodged in her throat. She would follow him anywhere.

"I'm right behind you," she told him truthfully. "I can keep up. I swear."

And she meant every word.

Levi George shoved his hand in his jacket pocket and fingered the knife he had secreted there. The director of the Navajo Department of Public Service would not normally carry a weapon. But the dog-lieutenant of the Skinwalker army, the right-hand man to the Navajo Wolf, most certainly would—and did.

"So…" Levi began, speaking with gritted teeth. "Let's go through it again. Tell me how you let an old grandmother and a baby slip through your fingers."

The two mercenaries standing in front of him knew they were in big trouble. One of them had already witnessed a partner lose his eyesight by means of a hot poker. And now these two were close to losing their lives.

George had met them at the right place and time this morning, as he had also done last night. He'd ordered this meeting for dawn at the old missionary cabin. And he'd fully expected them to bring the grandmother and the baby back with them. Either alive or dead. It didn't much matter which.

Instead, they'd arrived empty-handed.

"The females must've had a Brotherhood warrior

helping them," the slightly more talkative of the two said. "Had to be some kind of magic that spirited them away in the end, I'm guessing."

When the hired hand saw his boss's eyes narrowing, he hesitated. Then he visibly began to shake and whine.

"Just like we told you at that hogan when we met last night, we had no trouble at all locating where they'd spent a few hours in a…c-coyote den." He was stuttering with fear. "And when we followed their tracks through the cliffs and called you to meet with us, we were sure we were catching up to them. But…"

The man who had been speaking backed up a step, looking as if he was about to be sick. The director checked the other man's whereabouts, and found him with a hand on the door and ready to run.

These excuses were becoming tiresome. After he'd left them to search the area last evening, he'd spent the rest of the night putting the sacred map in its new hiding place. And it was well-hidden, if he did say so himself.

Now he was running short of time and patience. The director had only an hour or two left to get back to the Navajo Wolf with his story about losing the map. Any longer than that, and his dual personas as Skinwalker Dog and Navajo Nation Director would be permanently compromised. He himself would have no use left for a priceless map—because he wouldn't be alive.

He pulled the knife from his pocket, flipped it open and waved it in the air. "Explain one more time what happened before we met up last night. And try to sound like you have a modicum of intelligence."

Both men gasped. He heard a trickling noise and saw that the one by the door had wet his pants.

"Nobody moves," George threatened. "Not until I'm satisfied there is nothing left to be done."

"The Brotherhood must've helped them by magic," the other man cried. "Had to be. Like we told you, the old woman's tracks came right up to the edge of a slot canyon. She'd been traveling with a Navajo wearing moccasin boots. The male's boot prints moved away from the canyon, but the old woman's didn't. She had to have flown off the ledge—by magic."

The director sighed. "That's what you claimed last night. How can you be so stupid? Where'd you check after you searched that sheep herder's hogan?"

"Everywhere. We looked all night. Down in the bottom of the canyon. Up on the cliffs above them. There were three other hogans in the area, and we checked them all."

This was really more than he had time for. His life was on the line. So were theirs.

Without another word, he flicked his hand and the stiletto flew across the room. It caught the man standing by the door in the ear and pinned a piece of his flesh to the door behind him.

"Ow," the man howled. "You nearly murdered me. And I didn't do nothing. I didn't even say nothing to that pretty mama last night." He grabbed his ear and sniffed. "She was supposed to be mine, too. But I was doing what you said."

"What the hell are you babbling about? What woman?"

"That kid's mama we took off the bus. She was going to be mine when we got 'em both back to the cabin. Before she took off into the desert, that is."

The director was confused, but not much more than the guy whose ear was bleeding. "The woman you accidently took with the baby? She died days ago in that fire we set in the pipe cleft, remember? You've been dreaming. Maybe I ought to put you out of your misery."

He marched toward the hired hand, intending to retrieve his knife. Not much point in killing these two with a knife, though. It would take too much effort. He'd just shoot them both before he left for his appointment with the Wolf.

The man with the bloody ear saw the director coming his way and fell to his knees. "No lie. I wasn't dreamin' last night. She was there. In that first hogan. With the man. And I didn't touch her. Swear to God."

Stopping with his hand raised toward the knife, the director decided he had better hear more of this story. He turned to the other man as he ripped his blade out of the wood.

"What's he talking about?" he growled. "Your buddy is sniveling. What woman? And what man?"

"I told you," the other man whined. "There was a young couple in that sheep herder's hogan."

The director looked from one man to the other. His brain was swirling with images, none of them good.

He grabbed the shirtfront of the smelly guy with the bloodied ear. "You swear it was the same woman? Why didn't you say anything?"

"You said to keep quiet unless we found the old lady and the kid. They wasn't in there, so I shut up and went on looking for them like you said."

The bad feelings were getting worse. "So who was the guy? Not the one that supposedly died with her in the fire. That guy was a cop and one of the Brotherhood."

Both men shrugged.

This was beyond bad.

"Did he see me?" Panic was surging up the director's

throat and about to strangle him. "He didn't get a good look at me, did he?"

"Maybe," the stinking one whispered. "Maybe he stepped out of the hogan when you was in the light."

Hell. Hell. Hell.

He was a doomed man. If the Navajo Wolf didn't kill him, the Brotherhood would. And if somehow he scraped out of this mess alive, his political career would be over.

The baby and his appointment with the Wolf forgotten for the moment, the director changed his plans. "Get your gear," he shouted at the two goons. "We've gotta find those two before they leave the desert."

If he got lucky and reached them before they could tell anyone what they'd seen, he would be sure to kill that Brotherhood warrior and his rich woman. He would let his rifle correct the many errors these stupid hired hands had made.

Then he would fix the hired hands. For good.

Chapter 13

The morning had turned from pleasant to spectacular. Hunter took a moment and looked toward the deep blue skies and cotton candy clouds. A twinge of guilt over not having stopped to say his morning blessing still lingered in the back of his mind. But the beauty of his beloved homeland went a long way toward soothing the unease.

They were almost home free.

Having left behind the true desert, with its magnificent arches, spires and buttes, they were now moving through a canyon vibrant with rich red earth. A favorite place of Hunter's since he'd been a boy, the canyon held a wash with a trickle of water, even at this time of the year. Along the wash, next to the cattails and prickly pear cactus, grew tall cottonwoods whose leaves were just beginning to change to their familiar neon-yellow color for fall.

"Let's take one last break here, slick. You need another

drink of water." He stopped in the cool shade of the cottonwoods and pulled out a canteen.

Bailey hesitated, glanced over at him and then frantically looked around. "You sure it's okay? Where are we? I don't remember anyplace like this when those goons dragged Tara and me up and down cliffs." She was running off at the mouth, spilling out words faster than Hunter could keep up.

"Easy," he told her with a wide grin. "We're fine. We took a shortcut. And now we're only about a half hour from where I left my SUV. The cell phone is there and we'll be able to call for help."

She didn't look convinced, but she sat on a flat-topped boulder and accepted the canteen. "I don't know how you can be so calm. Skinwalkers…dark, evil witches that are real, could be following us. Probably *are* following us. In order to kill us. We could actually die!"

He sat beside her and put an arm around her shoulders. "Take that drink, slick. We're alive now, and we're going to stay that way. I've given our situation some thought—"

Frowning at him, Bailey lowered the canteen and interrupted him. "Thinking can't help us. These are *Skinwalkers!*"

"Shush," he whispered with a smile. "Shouting won't help, for sure. I've come to the conclusion the bad guys must still think we're dead. That they killed us in that cleft fire. We haven't seen any signs of them except for those two goons last night. And nothing on our trek this morning."

Hunter tilted his head to see her better. "We're golden, slick. It's all good. Baby Tara should already be back with her mom. And in another hour or so, you'll be on the phone to your father. We've made it."

Bailey smiled, but so halfheartedly it made him chuckle. "Really," he assured her softly.

Shaking her head in denial, she began to tremble. "Don't make promises you might not be able to keep. It's not your style, Hunter Long."

She'd been so strong for so long. Hunter had to give her the respect she deserved. Her courage had infuriated him at the beginning. Now he knew why it'd thrown him so far out of balance—because hers was so like his own.

That she was just now beginning to crumble, right when they were within sight of the end, made her seem much more human. Softer and decidedly feminine.

There were so many facets to the woman. Thousands. Millions, maybe. It would take a lifetime to learn them all.

But not his lifetime. It was a gut-wrenching thought, one he refused to dwell on.

They'd made it out of hell alive. They should be celebrating, not sitting here being either too scared to breathe, or else letting their brains fill with useless regrets over impossible futures.

He used his forefinger to gently lift her chin. "It's a promise I intend to keep. You will make it home alive."

As she searched his eyes for the truth, he lost control to a bigger truth that he'd hungered for but knew was a bad idea. Bending his head, he brushed her lips with his own.

Bailey was losing her mind. With her body awash in adrenaline and her heart stuck in her throat at Hunter's tender touch, she fell under the spell his lips were weaving.

This kiss was different. Slower, more intense. Was it a message from his heart about a love unacknowledged? A wordless assurance that he would keep her safe? Or maybe this was a world-class goodbye.

When he tunneled his fingers in her hair, she gave up

trying to outguess him. She slid her arms around his neck, closed her eyes and kissed him back with everything she had.

She opened her heart and allowed herself to feel the hidden places he'd locked inside himself. Places that had long been hurt and unloved. Breathing deeply, she filled with love. She so desperately wanted to soothe his old pains, to replenish and heal his hurting heart.

Love me back, Hunter Long. I beg you.

Too soon, he broke the kiss and leaned away. For just a second he looked stunned and lost, then he took a breath and crashed right back into their reality. His gaze flitted in every direction but hers as he checked the surrounding area.

"We have to get going," he said in a raspy voice. "It's time you went home." He stood and helped her get up.

The expression on his face was impossible to read. What had he thought of their kiss? Would it really be their last?

In silence, the two of them climbed the final mesa that Hunter claimed would lead to where he'd left the SUV. He was quiet, but appeared confident. She was still not so sure.

Something didn't seem right. It felt like someone's gaze was boring into the back of her neck. Were they being watched?

Shivering, Bailey tried to ignore how tired she was, how much she wanted to be back in civilization, and how badly her heart was aching. The very least she could do for Hunter's sake was to be strong.

"Hold it a sec," he said, suddenly going down on one knee when they came to a rise. "I can get a good view of my SUV from here. Let me check it out." He pulled the binoculars from his pack and focused on a spot down the hill.

Bailey stared over his head, trying to see what he saw.

But it was too far off and there seemed to be huge boulders in the way.

"My SUV looks the same as when I left it," he told her. "But the goons' Jeep is gone. Someone must've come for it. That isn't great news. Whoever took it away had to have seen my SUV parked behind it."

"What are we going to do?"

Hunter shook his head and stood. "Well, we're not going to walk into a trap. At least, you're not going to." He turned to her. "I've got to get to that cell phone."

"Where is it?"

"Under the passenger seat. Plugged into a battery pack. But I can't take any chances with you out in the open. You stay here. I'll get it."

"No." She was shaking again. "Don't leave me."

"You'll be safer here. If something happens to me, wait until dark and then go get that phone. The SUV isn't locked. If I'm not mistaken…" He looked up at the clear blue skies. "Yeah. The Bird People are here, watching out for us. If I run into big trouble, they'll get help and keep you safe. Don't worry."

"It's not me I'm worried about, Hunter Long. I can't let you get killed because of me. I can't. I want to go with you," she added with a small sob that verged on hysteria. "Maybe together we can work as a team. I'll cover for you."

The damn man grinned at her. "Sounds nice, slick. But I don't think so."

"I don't care what you think," she said with gritted teeth. "I'm pretty strong willed, if you hadn't noticed."

He chuckled, then gave her a wide-eyed look.

"Don't be cute," she argued. "This is serious. If you

leave me here, I'll just follow you. Where you go, I go. You are *not* dying without me."

Heaving a heavy sigh, Hunter rolled his eyes. "All right, fine. You can go a little closer. There's a boulder fairly near my SUV. You can hide behind that while I get the phone. But you'll have to carry my rifle. And agree to use it to protect yourself if necessary. Think you can do it?"

Bailey took a deep breath. "Of course," she managed to say, past the lump in her throat.

That brought yet another grin from Hunter. What kind of person smiled when his life was in danger?

"Okay, slick." He handed her the rifle, then put away the binoculars and turned to leave. "Let's get you home."

With one hand, Bailey hiked up the long, traditional skirt she was wearing, clutched the rifle with the other and began to creep over the edge of the ridge behind him. She was determined to find a way of keeping them both alive.

After all, the man up ahead was the one person she was destined to love forever. In sickness and in health. Until death do them part—and if it came to it, far beyond that.

Hunter twisted his head to check behind him. With her jaw set and her eyes blazing, Bailey was having no trouble keeping up.

Damn it. The adrenaline was obviously rushing through her veins and giving her a high, one better than any of her designer drugs.

She had no business heading off to potentially face her own death. He'd always thought of her as perfectly suited to the world of high fashion and global travel. But she was turning out to be more determined to survive and win than he had ever imagined she could be. Just like her father. Not letting anyone or anything stand in her way.

Why hadn't he seen that in her before now? Her flushed cheeks and the shimmer of expectancy in her eyes were turning him on.

Hell, he didn't want to feel any of it. Not now. Not ever.

The two of them silently crept into the narrow clearing between two boulders. A little while ago he'd given her last-minute instructions. Now he held up his hand to tell her to stop where she was. This was it. His SUV was parked on the other side of this rock.

He pulled her closer, into the shadow of the rough-sided boulder, and whispered in her ear. "Stay put and be ready to run."

"Run where? What's your hurry, Inspector Long?" The deep voice coming from over his shoulder had Hunter spinning toward the danger.

As he turned, he saw Navajo Tribal Police Director Levi George. The director was standing no more than ten feet away, with a rifle pointed straight at Bailey's head.

Hunter reached back and shoved her closer to the giant rock behind them, blocking her from the big man's view with his body.

Then he tried to dig from his stunned brain the sacred chants that he knew would protect them. But he couldn't think fast enough, so he went for his knife.

"Nuh-uh." Another male voice came from the opposite direction, right behind Bailey. "I wouldn't do that if I were you. Drop the knife, you Brotherhood devil. Drop it or I'll kill your girlfriend where she stands."

Glancing over his shoulder, Hunter saw one of the men from the hogan last night. The guy was standing close to Bailey, with a hunting knife aimed at her back. He wasn't the smelly one, but the one with a little more sense. It made Hunter wonder where Bailey's other suitor might be.

"If you want to give the woman a few more minutes of life, do what he says, Long. Drop the knife." Director George raised his eyebrows in rhetorical question as he swung the rifle away from Bailey and straight at Hunter's heart.

It was just far enough away from her to jump-start Hunter's brain. He began one of the sacred chants under his breath as he eased his knife to the ground.

"Stop that!" the director squealed. "Stop it now or I won't wait to get rid of you both."

"I'm just putting the knife down like you said." Hunter stopped saying the chants aloud and bent to place the knife on the ground. But his brain had cleared and he now stood ready to do battle with the evil.

The director grimaced. "You know what I mean. Don't try it again, I'm warning you."

"What difference does it make whether you kill us now or later?" Hunter asked. He faced him with a sneer and wondered if he could provoke the man. "What do you want, anyway?"

The safety on the director's rifle clicked off. Hunter realized Levi George was right on the edge. If he didn't kill them this instant, then he must want something…badly enough to make him hesitate. It was a crack in the armor that Hunter could use.

"I want respect," the director told him with a sniff. "From you. From everyone."

Hunter knew he had him.

"I'm sick to death of being everyone's whipping boy.

The Tribal Council treats me like a hired hand. And the damn Navajo Wolf thinks I'm his slave or something. To hell with that," he spat out. "I'm smarter than all of them combined. I'm going to be wealthy, far beyond your puny ideas of riches. I'm this close." He held up his thumb and forefinger, less than an inch apart.

The director lost focus for a second as he looked at his raised hand, and it gave Hunter a moment to study his face. His cheeks were pockmarked, his lips cracked and split. The guy was physically falling apart, exactly like the other Skinwalkers the Brotherhood had encountered.

It made Hunter wonder how sound the man's mind might be. But he kept his mouth firmly closed and let the director ramble on.

Levi George glared at him. "You doubt me? I've got the map hidden where no one but me will ever find it. What do you think of that?"

At the mention of the map, Bailey drew a soft breath behind Hunter. The sound made the director laugh.

"So *that* might make a difference in what you think of me, huh? Well, it should. Having control of the map is going to make me more powerful than the great Navajo Wolf himself."

Levi George had definitely gone over the edge of madness. Hunter had to find a way to save Bailey.

"What do you want from us?" he growled. The power he put into his voice took the big man back for a second.

"I don't want anything," the director replied. "But one of my hired hands let your woman get under his skin. He doesn't want his paycheck, he doesn't want to eat—nothing but her. So I made him a deal."

A chill went up Hunter's spine, but he straightened and

lifted his chin, looking down his nose at the other man. "She's not my woman. Why tell me? Just let me go on about my business."

Hunter could almost feel the anger sparking off Bailey behind his back. But he knew she wouldn't open her mouth. She was too determined to survive.

"Oh, come now, Long. I'm not dumb. I'm the one with the map, remember?" The big man shifted the rifle to his other hand, and wiped the sweat from his brow. "I'm offering you a deal for her, too. If you'll answer a couple of simple questions, I'll let you and Jacquez fight over her."

"What happens if I lose the fight?"

"Then Jacquez gets to keep her." The director scrunched up his nose in distaste. "Nasty fellow. I wouldn't want that fate for any woman I cared about."

"What happens if I win?"

Levi George smiled. "Then you get to say how she dies. A quick bullet to the head, maybe? Something easy and as painless as possible."

Where was Jacquez? Hunter would feel a lot better if he knew. "Yeah, okay," he told the director with a shrug. "I guess I'm in the mood for a good wrestle. I've got a whole lot of built-up stress that I'd just love to work off over that idiot's skull. Ask me your questions."

Jacquez stepped out from behind one of the boulders and stood next to his boss. His face and shirt were bloody, his ear was missing a big chunk of skin and his eyes had a glazed, burned-out expression.

But he was standing in a spot where he couldn't get a good look at Bailey. That was all that mattered for the moment.

"Very well," the director began. "Do you have your cell phone with you?"

"Huh? What do you want to know that for?" Hunter took a moment to think through his panic.

Did the man already know that his cell phone was in the SUV under the seat? Why had he bothered to ask the question? All George had to do was kill him and search his body for the phone to find out.

"That's my question, Long. Shut up and answer it or the deal's off."

Truth or dare. Hunter made his mind up which in an instant.

"I lost it. In the fire."

"You know…all I have to do is search you to find out if you have it."

"Yeah. So why'd you ask?"

"I wanted to see if you'd lie or tell me the truth."

"Well, you got the truth. What else do you want to know?"

"Have you spoken with any of your clan since last night?"

Hunter's mind was racing. What was the right answer to this question? What response would keep them alive the longest?

He flipped a mental coin in his head and picked the truth. "Nope. Haven't seen a single person at all while Ms. Howard and I have been out for our little stroll this morning. Why?"

That he'd been telling the truth this time must've shown on his face. The director studied him for a moment before smiling again.

"Fine, then," the big man said, and turned his head. "Jacquez, he's all yours."

Chapter 14

Hunter crouched and began bobbing and weaving. Bailey's blood pressure skyrocketed as she caught a glimpse of Mr. Smelly preparing to kill the man she loved.

How had they gotten to this point? And how the hell were they going to get out of it?

She held her breath, trying desperately to do everything the way Hunter had instructed. "If they find us, keep the rifle close to your side," he'd told her. "Don't give up without using it on them first," he'd added.

Well, she wanted to use the rifle right now. She'd never thought of herself as a killer before. Yet all she could imagine at the moment was how great it would be to put a bullet into Mr. Smelly's brain.

Hunter shot her one last cautionary glance, then turned to focus on his opponent. Bailey squeezed even tighter against the rock, keeping the rifle hidden between her body and the boulder. Hunter had said to shrink down and try to become invisible. This was the best she could do.

The heavyset man Hunter had called the director, the man who was the center of attention, seemed focused on the two men who were about to fight.

Bailey chanced a glance at the third man, who was standing close to her side and holding a nasty looking knife. He, too, appeared to be absorbed in watching two men try to kill each other.

She wasn't the least bit worried about Hunter being killed by Mr. Smelly. The man she loved was bigger, better and stronger than the goon who'd kidnapped her and Tara.

But when the fight was over, then what? She would have to be brave and keep her head. No matter what.

Mr. Smelly lunged at Hunter, who slid sideways and avoided contact. It was then that Bailey noticed the knife in Mr. Smelly's hand. She almost screamed at Hunter to watch out.

But she caught herself, closed her mouth and kept trying to disappear, as he'd told her. The fight wasn't fair, but then Hunter probably had known all along that it wouldn't be. Biting her lip, she watched as he wrenched Mr. Smelly's arm around and forced him to drop the knife.

She threw another quick glance at the director, who was scowling but still concentrating on the fight. He was the real danger, she knew. Any minute now he could change over into that horrible dog thing and kill them all.

Fighting off terror, Bailey looked back just as Hunter and Mr. Smelly both went to the ground, each desperately struggling for control of the knife. Mr. Smelly got to it first and quickly slashed at Hunter.

It was all she could do to keep down a hysterical gasp

as a sudden flash of red blood appeared on Hunter's cheek. But he showed no signs at all of being hurt. Never slowing, he simply forced the knife out of the other man's hand again.

They rolled on the ground and Hunter ended up on top, the knife in one fist and his other hand squeezing Mr. Smelly's neck. After a second, the goon grew weak and fainted.

Just then the henchman who'd been standing beside her suddenly yelled, "Enough! Game's over."

Without warning, he sent his knife sailing toward Bailey. The blue-steeled blade struck her smack in the upper arm. Shrieking at the intense pain, she ripped the knife from her flesh, dropped it to the ground and then grasped the rifle with her good hand, preparing to defend herself.

"No!" That angry shout came from Hunter, who raised his arm at the same time and sent the knife he held flying across the clearing.

Hunter's blade struck the man beside her with a deadly thud. She watched as the sharp steel buried itself deep in the man's neck. He took one silent step in her direction, then collapsed.

At first she was paralyzed with fright, sure that he would get up and finish the job of killing her. But he stayed down.

And as Bailey glanced up, the director raised his rifle and shot Hunter. Right before her eyes, the man she loved was blasted with a bullet to his chest.

Seeing Hunter's blood splattering everywhere, she felt her mind go numb, but her body reacted on instinct. Without really aiming, she raised the rifle barrel and pulled the trigger.

The director had turned in her direction and the bullet caught him in the gut. For a second he looked stunned as a blotch of red blood grew wider and wider across his shirt at the waist. The stench of gunpowder wafted through the air and choked her.

Raising his own rifle and pointing it in her direction, the man made an inhuman noise, then wailed, "I should've killed you first, bitch. You shot me, damn it. *Me!* I have the map. I'm this close…." He stopped speaking and fell to the ground in a heap.

Bailey dropped her gun and ran to where Hunter was lying. He was so still!

"Hunter," she cried. "Oh, God, no. Please don't leave me."

He blinked his eyes, and her heart started beating. But glancing toward the huge hole in his chest put her in a panic again. How could she save him?

"I'm not going anywhere," Hunter mumbled.

"Tell me what to do." She sniffed through the tears.

"Try to stop the bleeding," he moaned.

"Okay. Okay." She tore at the hem of her long skirt and managed to rip a few pieces off to use as a bandage. "How? Where do I put this?"

His whole chest seemed to be blown wide-open and was bleeding profusely. How was she going to stop the life from gushing right out of his body?

"Tie it around your arm," he managed to gasp. "Put pressure on the wound."

"*My arm?* What on earth are you saying?"

"Can't help you," he croaked in a hoarse whisper. "Stop the bleeding, then go for the phone. Call the Brotherhood."

His voice was getting weaker. His body shook with obvious pain.

"I can't leave you," she yelled. "What if you die while I'm gone?" Tears were rolling down her cheeks, but she hardly noticed.

"I'm not dead yet, slick," he whispered. Hunter gave a watery smile, and she tried to fight off her growing hysteria. "But it hurts like hell," he growled through tight lips. "Stick with the plan…go for the damn phone."

Bailey didn't much like helicopters on good days. But today, with one paramedic insisting she take pain medication and another in the back feverishly working over Hunter, she couldn't stand being in the confined space.

"I'm not taking whatever it is," she insisted forcefully to the hapless paramedic. "I want to be clearheaded until we get to the hospital. I need to find out how Hunter is before I—"

"Relax, Ms. Howard…uh, Bailey." The soothing words came from Hunter's brother, Kody Long, who was sitting facing her. "My brother is in good hands. And I performed a short curing ceremony for him before we took off. So please don't worry about him. You should do whatever the doctors tell you," Kody continued. "Your father is already at the Chinle Health Care Facility, waiting for us to bring you in. He won't be happy if you show up in shock and with your arm still bleeding."

Bailey had been stunned when Kody and the FBI had taken only five minutes to appear with a medevac helicopter after she'd called for help on Hunter's cell phone. Now the whole sky seemed alive with helicopters and the ground was crawling with federal agents and cops.

"They've stopped the bleeding and I'm not in shock." A millisecond later what he'd said sank in. "My father is there? Already?"

Kody gave her a thin smile. "He's been on the reservation for two days. We couldn't keep him away. He's not terribly happy with the Brotherhood at the moment. And

I'd rather not make him any madder. So if you don't mind, please do what the paramedic recommends."

She gritted her teeth, but tried to be pleasant to Hunter's only brother. "*No drugs.* Sorry. I can't."

Kody didn't look pleased. But he clamped his mouth shut and folded his arms over his chest.

"I'll talk to my father. It'll be okay."

"Good luck with that," Kody said, and then turned to look out the window.

Bailey knew how demanding and insistent her father could be. But he was a reasonable man. And he loved her above everything else. He would understand if she explained the situation to him.

"I do *not* understand you," her father muttered as he spun around to face her. "What were you thinking? You could've easily been killed. You actually came damn close."

"Dad, please," she replied in her most soothing voice. "I told you. I couldn't let Tara die."

She'd had twenty-two stitches sewn in her arm, and had been bathed, x-rayed and prodded. When she'd insisted and then begged to stay with Hunter in the E.R., the hospital nurses had finally convinced her that he desperately needed to remain calm. And he could best do that without her wringing her hands beside him.

The man she loved was currently in surgery, and had been for the last two hours. Waiting was taking a toll.

Her father had finally gotten her to eat something. But after managing to swallow some soup and crackers, she was back on her feet and pacing in a private waiting room. She'd refused to go any farther away than down the hall from Hunter while they worked to save his life.

She and her dad were standing toe to toe. He just couldn't seem to understand her motives.

"What was that child to you?" Luther demanded at last. "Why her? Why now? You've never done anything remotely like this in your entire life. And you couldn't have picked a worse time to be so heroic, either." He was shaking his head, his breathing was shallow and his eyes were growing wider and wider.

"Dad…" She was beginning to worry that he might be having a stroke.

"I sent the best tracker in the world out for you," he interrupted loudly. "And he finds you, saves you. And what do you do? You insist on staying out there! Running around the desert wilderness like some savage. I don't get it." Luther Howard seemed about to pop a blood vessel in his neck.

She watched him suck in a breath of air and then rush on, his face getting even redder. "Maybe you were just being a spoiled child again, if we're being absolutely honest about things."

He took another breath and blinked his eyes. "Bailey, the Brotherhood told me about the Skinwalker war." He'd begun speaking slowly, but in a much more somber tone this time. "I knew about the evil ones as a child, of course, but truly thought they were just legends. Now I have to believe it. You knew they existed when you took off, didn't you? You knew and yet you still insisted on playing games."

"It wasn't a game, Dad. It was deadly serious. But it was something I had to do."

Her father continued to shake his head. His whole body had tensed and was beginning to tremble. "I thought when you signed yourself into rehab, that you were finally going to start behaving like an adult. Your mother and I have always wanted only what was best for you. We didn't care what you did, just that it made you happy. But this…"

Bailey found herself shaking her head exactly as he'd been doing, so she put her arm around his waist and hugged him. "That was the point, Dad. You never expected anything from me, simply gave me whatever I wanted. I didn't know how to be responsible—to you, to society, to myself. Flitting around the world with every *thing* I ever wanted, but without a direction, did not make me happy. But I didn't know why. Now, I do know. Now, I'm finding out what's really important."

Her father slipped out of her embrace and sat down on one of the hard waiting room chairs. "You scared the hell out of your mother and me." His body slumped. "How is that being responsible?"

She had never seen him like this. For as long as Bailey could remember, her father had been bigger than life. He was soft and gentle on the inside, a man who loved his family and cared deeply about employees and stockholders. But his outside shell had always seemed hard and tough. Called the Navajo Shark in the world of business, he stood tall and fearlessly, an imposing figure that intimidated competitors.

At this moment, though, he looked more like a man who'd been through hell.

And she was the one who'd put him there. "I'm sorry. Really. I didn't mean to frighten you. If I could've called you to explain, I would have.

"But I couldn't walk away from the baby, Dad." Bailey stared deep into his eyes, willing him to understand. "I don't ever want to be the kind of person who would. I couldn't look you and Mom in the face."

"You explain it to your mother, then," Luther said with

a huge sigh. "You've caused her a lot of pain and you'll have to be the one to make her understand. Not me."

He sighed again and lifted his chin. "I've hired a Navajo woman to pack and move your grandmother. Though my mother is fighting the idea of leaving her home."

Shaking his head softly, her father took one more big breath. "As soon as the doctor says you are ready to be released, a plane will be standing by to take you home. Your mother is waiting at the house in the Hamptons."

Bailey sat down next to him. "I can't go yet." She knew he wasn't going to want to hear what she had to say, but she was determined. This was the path she had to take.

"I'll call Mom and talk to her. But I can't leave…at least not until Hunter is out of the hospital and is strong enough to say he doesn't want me to stay."

Luther Howard's eyes glinted, then softened. "I wondered if you two had rekindled your old flame. In my darkest moments, I was ready to blame him for keeping you out there in danger."

She shook her head so hard her whole body vibrated.

Her dad held up his hand. "Just in my darkest moments, honey. When I thought about it rationally, I knew damn well you would never let him or anyone else talk you into doing something you didn't want to do. That isn't who you are—and that isn't who Hunter Long is, either. He would never have put you in danger if you hadn't insisted."

"You knew I was that strong inside?" How could that be when she had never known it?

Her father nodded. "Certainly. You were that strong and independent at the age of three. I realize you sort of lost your way in the last few years. But who you are won't ever change."

The idea took her aback. But her next thought brought out another question.

"And how is it you knew what Hunter would do? For that matter, how did you knew he was the best tracker in the world?" When she hadn't even seen Hunter in eight years.

Luther Howard smiled at his only daughter. For the first time since she'd walked into the E.R. behind the stretcher carrying Hunter, his expression showed how much he loved her.

"Hunter Long was one of the few people who meant something in your life. I kept tabs on him over the years because I knew someday the two of you would have to finish what you started in college. Finishing what you start is who *both* of you are. I don't know if I'd call that determined—or plain stubborn."

She bristled at his description. But he just chuckled.

"All right," he finally agreed. "Call your mother. I'll arrange to get you a room near his. And I'll stick around as long as I can. I'm scheduled to be in China this week, but I guess it can wait awhile longer.

"Anyway, I still have to talk your *anali* into leaving Dinetah. She can't stay here alone. But she's just as stubborn...uh, determined as you are."

Her father's expression brightened a little. "Actually, I'd also like to stay to congratulate Hunter on putting up with you long enough to save your life."

"He's really hurt badly, Dad. I don't know if he's going to make it." A tiny sob leaked out without her permission.

Her father stood and took her into his embrace. "No question about that, honey. Don't give it a second's thought. He's got the best doctors. He's definitely going to make it."

* * *

"They say the tribal cop isn't going to make it," a female voice said from behind the alcove wall in the waiting room down the hall from the ICU. "I heard he has a punctured lung, and there's buzz about internal injuries."

Bailey's heart stood still, but her head felt as if it might explode at any moment. *No way!* Hunter couldn't leave her now.

She'd been buying bottled water from a machine, but she left it in the slot and turned to tell whoever had been speaking that she was wrong, that Hunter *would* live. Right then, Lucas Tso came down the hall with a Navajo man in a white coat, one she'd never seen before. The doctor turned into the ICU suite, while Lucas pulled her off to a quiet corner.

"That's our cousin Ben Wauneka," Lucas said softly. "He's a medical doctor, a crystal gazer and one of the Brotherhood. He's come to treat Hunter in the traditional way. We should wait with the family," Lucas continued. When she hesitated, he tugged on her arm. "In the waiting room."

She let him drag her away from the large, open ICU suite and down the hall. The waiting room was crowded with people. There was no place left to sit and hardly any way to talk over the din.

"Why don't we ask my father to help get us a private waiting room?" she whispered.

"These are Hunter's family members. And this is a private waiting room just for us."

"Really? Wow."

Lucas reintroduced her to Audrey Long, Hunter's mother, whom she hadn't seen in eight years. Mrs. Long in turn introduced her sister, Louise Ayze, her brother-in-law and her fiancé, who were all sitting with her. Hunter's brother, Kody, introduced his wife, Reagan, a pretty redhead holding their new baby boy in her arms.

So much family. It was intimidating. But Mrs. Long was kind, and went out of her way to make Bailey feel as though she belonged. As though everyone knew and accepted that she was part of the group who loved Hunter.

Another couple were standing off in a corner. Bailey recognized Michael Ayze, but not the beautiful blond woman with him. Lucas took her elbow and guided her over.

"Bailey Howard, please meet Dr. Tory Wauneka. She is the wife of our cousin Ben, and is also the plant tender for the Brotherhood."

"Dr.? Uh…plant tender?"

The blonde smiled. "Just call me Tory. It's a long story. I'm sure you'll hear all about it sometime. Maybe I'll be able to fill you in while we wait for Hunter's ceremony. That is, if you're really interested."

Bailey turned to Lucas. "Hunter's ceremony? What kind of ceremony?" All she could think of was that the man she loved must be dying and someone would be coming to say prayers over him.

Lucas didn't smile, but his expression softened. "It's true our cousin the warrior is very ill, but he will survive. I have seen it.

"But," Lucas hedged, "he must be cleansed with an Enemy Way ceremony. Michael Ayze will perform it soon enough. The Brotherhood will not lose Hunter Long."

Bailey shifted to address Michael. "What's an Enemy Way ceremony?"

"Our ancestors were great warriors," Michael began softly. "But it's not part of our religion to kill—even in battle. So when a warrior has had to take a life, he must be cleansed of the deed in an Enemy Way ceremony. It's one of our most ancient and least-used sings.

"It doesn't take days like most sings," he added in an afterthought. "But it will take many hours. The hospital has granted us permission to hold the ceremony in the ICU. There aren't any other patients at the moment. I'll begin as soon as Ben has finished his examination."

"Hours?" She didn't think she could stand not being able to see Hunter for hours.

"The Brotherhood will be there with him," Tory told her. "And Reagan and I will keep you company. We'll be here for you."

"But…" The tears came out of nowhere and she had to swallow hard to fight them off. "That's very kind of you."

She was really thinking she'd rather be with Hunter. What if he needed her? What if he was really dying?

"Part of learning our ways is understanding patience," Lucas told her. "If you expect to stay and be accepted, you must learn the traditions."

"Stay in Dinetah? Why would you say that? I haven't even decided myself yet."

Lucas actually smiled this time. "The decision has been made in your heart. Have the patience to let your head catch up."

Yeah, okay. Lucas was a little weird. But no one else seemed to notice or be bothered by what he said.

She would do as he'd suggested and practice having patience. Even if it killed her.

"I can't stand waiting," Bailey said four hours later.

Mrs. Long had taken her grandson and gone home with

most of her family to get a little sleep. They would return right after dawn.

Bailey had already heard Reagan's story about coming to the reservation to find her father, and running into Skinwalker troubles. Tory had told the story of how she'd been sent to the reservation to pay off her medical school loans. And the tale of how she'd learned to be the plant tender from an amazing woman named Shirley Nez, who had then been killed in a Skinwalker battle.

Their accounts had been filled with Skinwalker terror, but they were also stories about finding love. Both women had managed to keep Bailey from hysterics, but she'd never once stopped thinking about Hunter.

Reagan put an arm around her. "The waiting gets easier after a year or so. Are you hungry? Want a chocolate bar from the machine?"

"No, thanks." Whoa. Refusing chocolate? What a stunner. The addiction must be releasing its terrible grip on her body. Or else her brain had been fried with the worry about Hunter.

Reagan spoke to Tory over Bailey's head. "Kody said he's located a special satellite phone system for the Brotherhood to use—finally. I've been nagging him about it for months. To think that they've been relying on old-fashioned cell technology all this time—well, it's just beyond imagining. He's with the FBI, for pity's sake. He should know better."

Bailey knew the change of topic was meant to help her focus on other things. It was a nice thought, and she only wished she could.

Though in the back of Bailey's mind, right beside the worry about Hunter, a new thought began to emerge. These two new wives had both found ways of helping the Brotherhood. There must be something she could do, too.

But that idea would have to wait. Right now, all she wanted was to have Hunter healthy and back on his feet.

Chapter 15

Bailey leaned forward in her chair, easing toward Hunter's sleeping form. She gingerly picked up his hand, but he didn't stir in his hospital bed.

She couldn't help herself. Needing to touch him, needing to make a connection, she squeezed his fingers gently.

It had already been forty-eight hours since his operation, and this morning they'd moved him out of ICU. The many tubes in his arms were gone, but he still had a cuff attached, monitoring his blood pressure.

Hunter's body was healing, but Bailey's health was in question. She hadn't slept for over two hours at a time since they'd been brought to the hospital.

She'd tried. But until Hunter was on his feet, she didn't feel comfortable getting off of hers.

He looked so vulnerable like this, sleeping the day away. She understood that he'd lost a lot of blood and needed his rest. But she also knew there hadn't been any other internal injuries besides the broken ribs and the punctured lung. Thank heaven.

She would give anything if only he would wake up and talk to her. Talk to her about how much he loved her. Talk to her about a future.

An Anglo nurse bustled into the room. "There you are, Ms. Howard. I need to take your blood pressure and temperature. The doctors are concerned about you developing an infection. That arm wound isn't healing properly."

"Later, please," she whispered as she stood and moved away from the bed.

The nurse shook her head. "It won't do Special Investigator Long any good for you to make yourself sicker. You need your rest. Your body is straining to keep on running without a break. You have a room near here," the nurse added. "Why don't you use it?"

"I'm not leaving him unless he tells me to go."

Bailey relented enough to let the woman do her job and take her vital signs. However, she had no intention of moving far from Hunter's bedside.

With her immediate chores accomplished, the nurse tried one more time to convince Bailey to get some sleep. When that didn't work, the woman shrugged and left the room.

"Why aren't you sleeping?" Hunter asked in a low, raspy voice. "Still refusing to take the pain medication because of your addiction, slick?"

"Oh, Hunter. You're awake." She took three steps forward and picked up his hand again. Ignoring his question, she asked one of her own. "How are you feeling?"

When his gaze cleared enough to focus on her, what

Hunter saw threw him. Bailey's face was pale, her eyes sunken in her head. Under them were deep purple smudges. She'd never looked so haggard, not even in their worst moments after the shaft fire.

His gut wrenched at the sight of her. Raising his head and inching his shoulders higher on the pillow, he patted the bed beside him.

"I've been better," he said, and managed a grin despite the sharp pain in his ribs. "But I've also been worse. Come talk to me. Tell me what's going on."

She seemed hesitant to sit down. "You sure I won't hurt you?"

He held out his hand, but didn't answer. "Are you in pain? Is the cut on your arm bothering you?"

Shaking her head, she wrapped her arms around her waist in a gesture that said her pain was coming from a wounded spirit, not a wounded body.

He left his arm stretched toward her. "Sit down and tell me about what happened after I was shot."

"Don't you remember?" Bailey finally eased down beside him.

"It isn't clear. I want to hear it from you."

"Well… I was so scared. I thought…I thought you were dying. I shoved a wad of material under your shirt against the wound and ran for the phone. It was—"

"Before that." There was something she was avoiding. Something she needed to say.

"You mean when the knife cut my arm? I didn't have time to think about it." She let a pensive silence linger between them for a few moments.

"Slick, I think there's something else. What about when I killed that goon with my knife? Did that bother you?"

"The guy deserved it. He tried to kill me," she said with a tilt of her chin. "You should've killed Mr. Smelly, too. He was even worse. He tried to kill *you*."

"What happened to him?

She actually smiled, but it was a vacant smile that didn't suit her face. "When the FBI arrived, our old buddy was sniveling and whimpering incoherently. He wasn't physically injured so much as he was out of his mind. They tied him to a stretcher, to wait for a second medevac helicopter. But when those medics finally arrived," she continued, "they found him dead."

"Dead? What happened?"

Bailey shrugged a shoulder. "No one knew until they had an autopsy done yesterday in Farmington. Apparently he'd been bitten by some poisonous insect."

"Skinwalkers." The word popped out of his mouth. It wasn't a question.

"I guess." She raised her chin, looking much like a defeated warrior who refused to give up until beaten into the ground. But her eyes burned with some still-unspoken horror. He wished she would let him take her in his arms and make whatever it was go away. She was holding back, however, and that made him even more concerned about the welfare of her spirit.

"Bailey," he whispered. "What happened to the director?"

Before he'd even finished the question, she was shaking her head, begging him with her eyes not to ask.

"I… He…" At last her shoulders slumped, her face crumpled and tears welled up, cascading down her cheeks. "I shot him," she said through huge gulps. "Oh, Hunter, I actually killed a man."

For a moment he felt a blast of pure panic. What could he say? She needed a curing sing. But it would take time to set one up. How could he help her right now?

Then he looked into her tear-streaked face and knew immediately what she was in need of first. Pulling a few tissues from the box on the nightstand with his good hand, he helped her wipe her nose.

"Why don't you lean back here beside me for a moment," he said as gently as possible. "It's okay to cry it out, slick. No one will know." Ignoring his complaining ribs, he inched over in the bed a little to give her room.

He used his good arm again to tug her closer. She slowly complied, lying down and curling up in a tight ball next to him.

"Listen to me, Bailey," he whispered into her hair. "You didn't kill a *man*. The director was a Skinwalker. They've taken the path away from humanity. Away from their clans and everything it means to be Navajo."

Her sobs slowed, and he relaxed, nestling closer to her body. The warmth and the sweet smell of her felt so right that his own tension began to dissolve.

"Remember, it was either our lives or a monster's existence," he murmured. "You did what you had to. You did the right thing."

She didn't move and seemed to be quieting down, so he buried his nose in her hair and closed his eyes. Understanding what she was going through helped him to know what she needed the most. Many times he'd been exactly where she was.

"Rest, slick," he said in the quietest whisper imaginable. "Go to sleep and let it go. I'm here. And I'm not going anyplace."

* * *

For six straight hours, he fought off nurses and hospital administrators so she could sleep in his bed. Her doctor finally relented and allowed it, because she'd needed the rest so badly. And through all the negotiations, Bailey never even stirred.

The next day, however, she was awake and stirring magnificently—and in his opinion, most annoyingly, too.

"Just do it for me," he muttered through tight lips. "It's important for you to find balance again."

"I don't want to leave you until you're on your feet."

He gave her a furious glare. "I'm up, damn it. See?"

Maybe he was bent over like an eighty-year-old, but he was out of bed and walking around, finally. And as soon as he could manage to escape the nurses, he would be long gone from this place. He'd had enough of being prodded and poked. His body would heal just fine outside.

"You need the curing ceremony as soon as possible, slick," he argued. "Michael Ayze has agreed to stop everything else so you can be cured of your demons. He's one of the best singers in Dinetah. And I'll try to get there later for support. But you need to start right away."

"I don't know. Where is my sing supposed to take place?" She looked unsure, and the expression on her face was *so* not like the Bailey he knew.

Hunter was more certain than ever that she needed to be cured. And soon.

"Your father has arranged to hold the sing out at your grandmother's ceremonial hogan. Family support is a big part of what it takes to be cured. But you'll also have the Brotherhood and my mother there to see you through the ceremony. It'll be fine, slick. Really. You need this so you can go on with your life—your future."

"But what will I have to do? I don't know anything about sings."

"Just let it happen. Pay attention to Michael. He'll help you."

"Well, all right. But what about you? Will you be okay if I go?"

His heart squeezed in his chest. He'd been preparing himself for her to go almost since the minute he'd seen her again. He knew her leaving was the right way. The only way. But is was also the worst thing he could possibly imagine.

"I'll be fine," he said as he turned his back to her. He couldn't bear to see her walk away, but he knew it was for the best.

"Hunter…?"

"I need to take a shower. My hair still smells like smoke and I want to clean up," he told her, trying his best to sound as though it meant nothing to him. "You go on. I'll catch up to you tonight."

He began shuffling off toward the bathroom and heard her turn to leave. Holding his breath, he waited until he heard the door softly close behind her.

Bent double by the powerful aching in his chest, he folded his arms tightly around his middle. He could swear it felt as if his heart had walked right out that door with her. And there was nothing he could do. No medicine or sing that could cure him.

Bailey waited for Michael Ayze to finish speaking to her father. She absently stared at her fingertips and suddenly realized how chipped and broken her nails had become.

Her feet were callused. Her hair would need an all-day salon treatment before she could get a comb through it again. She hadn't shaved her legs in two weeks, and there were purple or yellow bruises on every inch of her body.

And it was only when she stopped to concentrate like this that she even remembered to care.

"Are you about ready, Bailey?" Michael took her elbow and began leading her toward the empty ceremonial hogan.

"What are you going to do? How does this sing work?"

Michael stopped and studied her face in the low light of dusk. "You and I will be alone in the hogan, with only the fire for lighting. There are many chants and herbs I'll be using, but you just sit quietly and pay attention. Your friends and family will be out here, standing by if you need them. But you'll have to trust me completely.

"The most complicated part of the ceremony is when I draw sacred paintings in the sand. They can take days to complete."

He watched her expression as she gave him her most skeptical look. "I'll try to speed it up some for you," he told her with a low chuckle. "And we'll stop to take a break in the middle."

"If the sand paintings take so long, what do you do with them when the ceremony is over?" she asked. "If you're such an artist, will you sell them?"

Shaking his head, Michael began moving toward the hogan again. "That would be sacrilegious. The paintings must be destroyed for the cure to be complete."

"Oh." She stopped before entering the formidable-looking, eight-sided building. "I guess I don't really under-stand this whole balance thing. I suppose Anali's lessons when I was a kid didn't stick with me."

Michael stopped just short of the doorway and placed his hands on her shoulders. "To live a life of beauty and balance is what all Navajos strive for. The core concept is about one being present in this world. It's about having a sense of community, of belonging somewhere. And about knowing, without considering your bank accounts, that you have worth. That whoever you are, whatever your talents, you are a needed and wanted member of the Dine."

Well, it was true. The one thing she wanted most in the world was for Hunter to need her.

She took a big breath and forced a smile. "Okay, then. I guess I'm ready. Let the sing begin."

Two mornings later, Bailey emerged from the ceremonial hogan and faced the rising sun. A fleeting thought about her appearance came to the forefront of her mind.

If she'd imagined she looked ragged before the ceremony, the sight of her now would probably scare away little children. Her face was streaked with charcoal stripes, put there by Michael during the sing. She hadn't had a shower in two days. And the remains of several hastily eaten meals stained the front of the deep maroon skirt and blouse that Mrs. Long had given her to wear when she'd begun the ceremony over two days ago.

Her hair smelled of smoke from the fire pit. Her feet and nails were caked with sand. But somehow, the way she looked mattered even less to her now than it had before.

Michael appeared, ducking out of the ceremonial hogan, and invited her to join him in saying prayers to Dawn Boy. Her father and grandmother and most of her new friends in the Brotherhood had already begun. The ⁀ n stood at the rim of Anali's maternal clan's green valley. They were facing the East and the beginning of a brand-new day and life.

Though she'd forgotten the words for the morning chant, Bailey went to stand with her father and friends. Michael loaned her a few grains of pollen. And rather than panic that she wouldn't know what to do with the stuff, she accepted the pollen and found peace in knowing no one would care if she threw it in the air a moment too late.

She felt different from before. Deep inside she was different—yet familiar.

Michael had taught her that the word for what she was feeling was *hozho,* walking in beauty with the environment. Finding yourself at peace. Being content and free from worry.

Bailey looked up at the wooded hillside behind her grandmother's cabin, then let her gaze sweep toward the empty sheep pens and wildflower-filled pastures below. They were standing at the edge of her clan's heritage, on the talus slopes of the great Colorado Plateau. Farther to the east, through hazy filtered sunlight, she could see the flat, semi-arid plains of the Two Grey Hills area.

Beyond the town stood what looked like a bluish lump off in the distance. She knew that was Shiprock Mountain, a favorite place of hers as a girl.

The view reminded her of a thousand echoes of memory from tens of generations of her ancestors who had stood at this same place and said their morning prayers. She belonged here.

Originally, she'd imagined that Hunter would have to leave Dinetah and follow her back to her home if they were to have a future together. Now she knew better. *This* was her home.

When the prayers were completed, Bailey found herself being congratulated on finishing the two-day curing ceremony. Anali was the last one to give her a hug.

"I knew you would come home, daughter," her grandmother whispered. Bailey realized the old woman was using the generic term for "young woman in the family," the same way the term "grandmother" was used out of respect for any older woman.

Her grandmother was nearly blind, but in the morning's brilliant sunlight her eyes burned brightly as she smiled at Bailey. "This is your place—the place of your tomorrow. Your children's children will know the beauty you behold."

"Oh, Anali, I'm so sorry you're sick," Bailey's heart was broken as she thought about her grandmother's incurable disease. "But you have to leave your cabin. Dad says you have to go to a nursing home. You can't stay here."

Her grandmother just smiled again and took her hand. "Come with me, child. I want to show you a good spot to build a new house. My mother's mother expected me to build in that place, but my time has come and gone. I will not be leaving the house of my mother's family before my earth years are over.

"Your man will make a home with you under the same cottonwood tree that my grandfather planted in my name. I know it will be so."

Bailey shook her head, but let her grandmother lead her up the slope. She hadn't said anything to Anali about Hunter. The sick old dear must be seeing something in her mind that didn't exist.

Bailey blinked back the tears, knowing that most of what her grandmother had said was coming from the disease in her mind. One day soon Bailey would bring

Hunter out here to see her clan's heritage and tell him of her newly discovered peace. But it would be too late for her grandmother to talk to him about new homes under the cottonwood trees.

That sad thought put a gray cast to a morning that had once dawned bright and blue and so full of the future.

Chapter 16

"You didn't come. I waited for you. But you didn't come." Bailey's voice sounded from over his shoulder. She must be standing down the hill, in the direction of his mother's house. "I haven't even heard from you in days."

Hunter turned and lifted his hand to shield his eyes from the bright morning sun. "Sorry." It was all he could manage, since his breath had pushed out of his lungs at the mere sight of her standing there.

Why had she come?

Hunter had deliberately kept busy, waiting for her to leave Dinetah and go home with her father. He'd hoped she would be too busy to find out where a dull half-breed like him lived. Who would've thought she'd go to this much trouble just to tell him off?

"Kody told me you were living in the hogan he'd built for himself two years ago. He said the place was up the hill from where your mother used to live—the house where he and Reagan and the baby live now. It's nice up here in the pines."

Turning his back to her again, Hunter hefted the ax and grasped it firmly in his palm so he could cut up the firewood. It was good, honest physical labor. The kind his body had been dying to do since he'd gotten out of the hospital.

"Do you think you ought to be doing that?" she asked.

He ignored her question and refused to turn around. "I heard your sing went well," he said instead. "Why are you still on the reservation? I thought you'd be back at your favorite shoe store by now."

Okay, that was a little harsh. But damn it. Why had she come all the way out here just to drive him crazy?

Bailey stayed quiet for so long that he lowered the ax and prepared to turn and apologize for being such a bastard.

"You were going to let me leave without saying goodbye?" she murmured in a low voice. "Without saying...anything?"

He knew this was going to be a bummer, but he had to turn around and take his punishment. Though, really, he wasn't too sure why the *yei* were punishing him this way. What had he done to deserve it?

Turning as slowly as he could, he expected to see a bruised expression on her face. He thought he'd probably hurt her feelings somehow, and he didn't want to face it.

All he wanted was for her to go away and leave him alone. Alone with memories. Alone in his pain.

But when he looked at her, what he saw was a sophisticated woman who was strong and independent. Instead of hurt and anger in her eyes, something calm and cool and loving was written all over her face.

A light sensation took over, where all his pain and

anguish had been only a moment before. He felt completely comfortable in her presence. She was everything to him.

But then he looked again and saw the way she was dressed. The expensive suit and the tasteful earrings. And his heart sank.

She was the sun, all bright and shiny and golden. His dark half moon could never hope to keep up. The two of them were merely destined to eclipse one another periodically in this lifetime.

He could never give her anything—never even travel in her universe.

"Didn't figure you'd be sticking around Navajoland long enough to notice whether one half-breed waved goodbye or not," he said without thinking. "I imagined, once you had your curing ceremony, that you'd be long gone."

It wasn't what he'd wanted to say. But telling her the truth, that seeing her leave was too devastating and way too hard for a mixed-up, worthless jerk like himself—telling her that truth was totally impossible.

Just turn around and go, beauty.

"You won't care if I leave or stay, then?" Bailey smiled, but the casual move cost her something.

He shrugged a shoulder and lowered his eyes. Damn the man. What had happened to change everything?

Her whole body felt the sting of his rejection. Still, she'd glimpsed a flash of something in his eyes. And she would swear it was the love she'd hoped to see.

So, ignoring the growing tear in her heart, she plowed ahead. "I'm considering staying in Dinetah. But my father is freaking out about it because of the Skinwalker war. I thought maybe you'd have an idea of how to convince him. Or maybe be able to come up with something I can do to help the Brotherhood. It would be great to say I'm needed here."

Flashing gray eyes, set deep in an angular face, looked down to where she stood. "No clue. In fact, I'm with your father. You need to leave. It can be dangerous in Navajoland."

She fisted her hands on her hips so he wouldn't see them trembling. "I'm not going, Hunter. The Brotherhood can protect me, teach me how to protect myself. I don't have anything the Skinwalkers want anymore. I should be safe."

"If you'd already made up your mind, why did you come to me?"

"Damn you, Hunter Long." She felt like stomping her foot, but refused to revert back to her old ways. "I've idolized you for nearly ten years. I've continually made excuses for the way you treated me and for the way you always keep your feelings to yourself. In my head, I gave you a pass for not jumping feet first into our affair and becoming as involved with me as I was with you. I tried to be understanding, and I gave you space because of your father.

"But now…" She suddenly couldn't think clearly—not when her fingers had curled at the memory of exploring his fine masculine chest. And not when she puddled at his feet at the mere sight of those incredible eyes.

Swallowing the huge lump that had formed in her throat, she tried to go on. "You *were* involved with me—in a big way out in the desert. Oh, I let you wallow in your self-pity and hatred. But I did it because I love you and thought that what you needed was to get it out of your system and love me back."

"I know…." he agreed. "But I haven't changed at all. I can't be what you need. Sorry. Guess I'm a selfish bastard."

"You *are* selfish. You're selfish because you refuse to let yourself need me. I imagined all along that it was *me* that needed *you*," she added, her voice growing ever more shrill. "Then I had the sing and realized what I really wanted was for *you* to need me. But no...you *like* wrapping yourself in guilt and pain. You refuse to allow anyone to love you."

God, her voice was sounding like what her mother would call a low-class shopgirl's. It embarrassed Bailey, so she turned to walk away—to calm down.

But the rest of the words just had to be said. She swung back and shook her finger at him in a most unNavajo way.

"I love you, Hunter Long. I will forever. But you are not in harmony. Wake up. You insisted that I go through a curing ceremony, but it's you who needs to find *hozho*. Your spirit is in so many different places, you'll never be in balance.

"Please," she added with a sigh. "You need bigger medicine...a stronger sing. Something. Wake up and live."

With that, she did turn, swiped at her eyes and headed down the hillside toward her car. She was starting a brand-new life here in the Navajoland of her ancestors, but a part of her heart would be left behind.

Hunter was holding her heart in his hands, his choice to throw away or not. And he always would.

Please don't go, beauty. Hunter's spirit was saying the words that his mouth refused to set free.

As he watched her walk to the bottom of the hill and drive away, the silence around him seemed complete. Silence was a good thing, right? Everyone knew Navajos lived great distances from each other because they didn't like noise.

Once, he'd craved silence. Back then his mother's screams and his father's terrifying grumbling had echoed in his ears. But that was long ago. Today he would much rather hear the soft sighs and sensual moans coming from the warm woman lying beside him. As long as that woman was Bailey.

He sat down on the woodpile, bowed his head and let himself cry it out. He wept for all the years he'd wasted away from Bailey. He wept because he'd turned into an arrogant bastard who was as demanding and emotionally distant as his father. He wept for beautiful Bailey, who didn't deserve to be ignored—who deserved someone that would cherish her for all the wondrous things she was.

Striking out blindly at his own ignorance, Hunter accidentally hit the ax's sharp-edged blade with his hand. He stared down at the oozing red wound and expected to feel anger as he normally did at the sight of blood.

But it didn't come. Instead, he just felt empty.

"Will that cut need suturing?"

The unexpected male voice surprised him. He looked up to find his cousin Lucas Tso standing next to him.

Damn, but the guy was more than a little weird. Spooky sometimes, too.

"Why have you come, cousin?" he asked, sincerely shocked to have Lucas visiting him in the middle of the day. "Is there Skinwalker trouble?"

"You needed me. So I am here," Lucas said cryptically. "But you didn't answer me about the wound. Should we take you to the health care center?"

"I don't think I'll be ready to see that hospital again for

a good long while," he said as he surreptitiously hid one last sniffle. "Since you're already here, though, you can help me clean out the cut. Then it'll be just fine."

Without another word, Lucas spun and headed for Hunter's hogan. "Was that the Howard woman I saw leaving?" he asked over his shoulder. "How is she doing since her sing?"

"She seems terrific," Hunter replied, while trying to catch up. "Says she's going to be staying in Dinetah." It was the most he could manage to say about Bailey without totally breaking down again.

Lucas reached the doorway first, stopped and turned back. "She is right, you know."

"Huh? What does that mean?"

"She's right about the 'needing.' A person *takes* to become stronger. But they *give* to make their lover stronger."

Hunter held his bloody hand in the air and opened the door with the other. His cousin's words were too obtuse to believe. It sounded as though Lucas had been standing right beside him while Bailey had said her piece.

"Why did you really come here today?" Hunter asked, instead of talking about the woman who had just stormed out of his life.

"I told you. I came because you needed me."

"Yeah, so you said. But how the hell did you know what I needed?"

Lucas nodded toward Hunter's cut hand. "Don't you need my help?"

Sometimes his cousin was absolutely impossible. But his words about Bailey were starting to make some sense.

Sighing, Hunter decided he would have to talk it all out with someone. Maybe Lucas was as good as anyone.

Or maybe, if Hunter gave himself another thousand years or so, he would be able to figure it all out alone.

"I'll give it a little consideration," Michael said. "What did Hunter say when you asked him?"

Bailey had come to the Dine College in Tsaile in order to seek out Michael Ayze's advice and opinion. But now she wondered if she'd done the wrong thing.

"He isn't my husband, my father or my boss," she answered with a sarcastic roll of her eyes.

When Michael continued to stand behind his desk, quietly staring at her, Bailey was sorry she'd opened her mouth and inserted her foot. But she took a deep breath and tried a tight smile. "Sorry. I'm a little tense lately. Hunter wants no part of me at the moment. He didn't have any answers for me, either—just said I should leave Dinetah."

"But you don't want that," Michael added without asking. "You want to stay in Navajoland, helping the Brotherhood. But without being close to Hunter. Is that what you're saying?"

She shrugged. "I guess so, yeah. At least, I know I intend to stick around Dinetah. It's his choice about our being close or not."

When Michael raised an eyebrow, she quickly added, "I *intend* to find something to do to help the Brotherhood. I have two trust funds, both worth millions. And I know I can talk my father into setting up a secret foundation so we can funnel money into the fight against the Skinwalkers."

Michael smiled and came from behind his desk. "Take a walk with me? The weather's always nice this time of year, right before fall."

Bailey had a feeling there was another lesson he wanted

to give her. She'd decided the outdoors was a wonderful place to be in Navajoland, so she gladly went along.

Not entirely positive one more lesson was really necessary, she steeled herself to pay attention, anyway. Another thing she'd noticed was that the Dine always told a legend or a story before coming to the point. She was starting to enjoy taking the time out to listen, but wished it didn't have to happen today.

Once they were outside, Michael went to a secluded grove of live oaks and sat down on a bench. It was a beautiful day, clear and blue, with nature preparing to hold its breath for the start of winter.

"Mind if I give you one more lesson about balance and harmony?" he asked softly. "I mean, if you intend to stay with your people, perhaps you should learn as much as you can about their traditional values."

"All right. I guess it couldn't hurt."

Michael's eyes crinkled in a warm half smile. "Don't take what I'm saying the wrong way, then. But you should know that most traditionalists believe it's unhealthy to be famous, and that it's wrong to have a lot more things than you need."

"What? But...but—"

He held up a hand, indicating she should hear him out. "The reasoning seems to be that having too much for yourself must mean you are not taking care of your relatives. Not always true, I know. But it's a firmly held belief, at least among the elderly and other traditional thinkers.

"I know of a Navajo man who became a rodeo circuit star," Michael added as an example. "He was making lots of money, had lots of fame. But his guilt drove him to quit and come home."

"There are several really wealthy Navajos in the world," Bailey argued. "Like my father."

Michael nodded. "Luther Howard has always tried to stay out of the limelight, though, and has done everything he can to take care of his mother's clan.

"But he doesn't live in Dinetah, Bailey. Leaving is where he first turned his back on tradition. I'm guessing your father doesn't feel the least bit guilty about his money, either."

Bailey managed a smile. "I doubt it. But are you trying to tell me that I should give up all my money if I want to live in Dinetah and get along with everybody?"

"No, not at all," Michael told her. "In fact, the Brotherhood would be grateful to become the recipients of a new foundation. We could use a lot more technical equipment, for one thing. And I think the time may be coming when a few of us will need indefinite leaves of absence from our jobs in order to fight the Skinwalker war full-time. Extra funds would make that a whole lot easier."

"I hear a *but* in the middle of all you said."

Michael's smile was wide this time. "Smart woman. It's okay if you have the money to take care of the Dine and use it for that purpose. It's just *not* okay to flaunt it. If you're going to reside here in Dinetah, you should try to live life in the same way as your neighbors.

"Not necessarily by herding sheep or weaving rugs," he added with a chuckle. "But in living quietly. The People do not live in huge mansions. Or wear designer labels."

She looked down at her Gucci suit and her Prada heels.

"I hadn't given clothes any thought. This is what I own."

"You don't own jeans?"

"Sure I do," she said with a shrug. "But they're all designer label, too. I guess I can buy some regular jeans, and maybe my workout shoes would do until I can find out what everyone else here wears on their feet."

"Good idea. I have a feeling that Hunter would also appreciate seeing you in more casual clothing."

"You think?" Bailey wasn't so convinced. She didn't believe Hunter noticed what she wore at all, he was so wrapped up in his own troubles. "Living quietly and setting up a foundation will be easy for me," she told Michael. "But I want to do more for the Brotherhood. I want to fight. There must be something—"

"You can't be a warrior, I'm afraid. The Brotherhood members are all medicine men. What do you know how to do?"

"Nothing. But I'm smart. I can learn anything. And I'm tough. I put myself into rehab when things got bad, and I made it out to the sober side.

"And I lived through being kidnapped and having Skinwalkers after me. Those things should count for something."

"They do. I have one suggestion."

"I'll try anything."

Michael's expression turned serious. "Ben Wauneka was talking to me the other day about starting a counseling program for methamphetamine users—mostly for our young men who would otherwise be easy targets for Skinwalker recruitment. Once they become addicted, the young people will follow anyone who promises them more meth. It's an easy Skinwalker lie to pretend their powers are exactly like a meth high. Think you would be interested in setting up a program to keep young Navajos from the dark side?" he asked.

"Definitely. It would mean a lot of work, but I know

counselors back at my old rehab center that would be willing to advise us on the best way to go."

The two of them discussed how a center would work, and who at the Navajo Nation Department of Behavioral Health might be willing to help set it up on the rez. Bailey was so thrilled to find something she was qualified to do in the Skinwalker war that she almost forgot all about the gaping hole in her heart. The one Hunter's rejection had caused.

Almost. But the dull ache stayed put, lying in wait for her quiet moments, no matter whatever else she thought or did.

Hunter pulled his SUV to the side of the gravel road, right around the bend from Bailey's grandmother's homestead. For several weeks now he had tried to avoid the growing certainty that seeing Bailey was the only way he could continue living his life.

He and Lucas had spent days talking about many things. They'd had discussions about each of their strange dreams of Hunter's dead father, but neither came up with a reasonable explanation. In the end, they could only decide that both of them would remain open to the truth.

They also talked about Hunter's fears of not being able to control his anger. And about his anxieties concerning the wide differences between his and Bailey's lives.

Lucas's words had helped him see past the clouds of fear, and helped him see himself more clearly.

Hunter had also heard from Michael about Bailey's wanting to help the Brotherhood. He'd been surprised and humbled to hear of her strength of purpose.

Finally, he sat alone and remembered how proud he'd been of her stance against the Skinwalkers, and of how she'd fought so hard to save the baby.

Miserable and so lonely he thought he might die, Hunter had at last made a decision. He knew she was a strong, amazing woman. Today might be the day to find out if she also had a generous and forgiving spirit. He thought she did. At least, he hoped so.

Taking a deep, cleansing breath, he put the SUV in gear and headed off to find out what she thought.

Bailey thought she heard someone calling her name. She stopped reading aloud to her grandmother for a moment and lifted her head to listen.

"Yes, child, a person has arrived for a visit. His spirit calls to yours, not to mine."

"Do you really hear that noise? It seems so far away. How can you tell whether it's a man or woman? It's probably just the wind."

"The voice is in your heart, Granddaughter. I didn't hear anything. Go accept your destiny."

Bailey sighed. It had been a couple of days since Anali had spoken any words at all, and longer than that since she'd recognized the faces of her loved ones. This afternoon the older woman knew Bailey, but was imagining things. Her illness must be growing much worse.

"I'll just finish this chapter for you first."

Her grandmother shook her head and put her hands over her ears. "Go now."

"All right. I'll check. But if no one is there, I'll come right back inside and finish this for you."

Bailey set the book down and went to find her grandmother's nurse. Her father had brought in a house trailer and put it behind the cabin so that the full-time Navajo nurse he'd hired could live close by.

Between Bailey and the nurse, her grandmother was getting good care and would be able to stay in her home until the end. But it was heartbreaking for Bailey to see someone she loved deteriorating.

"There is a young man in an SUV, waiting to be invited inside," the nurse said when Bailey found her.

"Oh?" Bailey went off to see who had come, wishing she could be more like a real member of the Dine. A Navajo raised here would've been aware that someone was waiting.

When she saw the visitor, she stilled. Her feet refused to carry her any farther.

Hunter got out of the SUV and walked in her direction. "I understand you're living here and caring for your grandmother. I was wondering if you might be available to go for a drive."

"That should be okay. Anali's nurse is with her now."

He helped Bailey climb into his SUV, and they drove off through a part of the Lukachukais Mountains that didn't seem familiar to her. When they rounded a curve, she suddenly recognized where they'd been heading.

"I remember this place," she said. "You brought me here once a long time ago."

Hunter nodded and pulled the SUV to a stop. "It's my favorite place. The one where you can see to all four states of the Four Corners."

She got out and went over to the edge of the cliff. "It's still as beautiful as it ever was."

"And you're still as beautiful as ever, too."

She turned around and found him standing a few feet away. Those dazzling steely eyes of his were clouded by an internal struggle of some kind. Bailey tried not to get her hopes up.

"I'm glad you seem happy and healthy," he said. "I also like the new look."

She'd totally forgotten about the work jeans and flannel shirt she had on today. "I like it better, too. At least it's more comfortable. But my mother had a fit over my appearance the last time she was here to visit." Bailey shrugged. "She got over it."

"You don't leave the reservation even to see your mother?"

Bailey shook her head. "I'm needed here. Mother doesn't really mind coming to see me. It keeps us all out of the media spotlight."

"You've changed, Bailey." He crossed his arms over his chest and stared.

"Just on the outside." She began to fidget under his scrutiny. "What was it you wanted, Hunter?"

"I've thought a lot about what you said the last time. About my refusing to allow anyone to love me."

Bailey felt the spark of hope jumping to life.

"You were right," he told her. "I didn't want you to be in love with me. I tried to stay away from you, but that didn't work out. I had to come for you, anyway."

She smiled, but his expression was so serious that all the humor rushed away.

"I would've come for you eventually, even without the Skinwalkers," he admitted. "Whether my brain wanted it or not. I need you. I need you to help me stay in the present. To keep breathing. I always have."

She opened her mouth to say something, but the words refused to come.

"Lucas helped get my head straight," Hunter admitted. "I'd thought you were the sun and far out of my league. But now I see differently."

What was he waiting for? He should be walking over here and kissing her senseless. Her knees were growing too wobbly to hold her.

"Will you give me another chance? You need me, too. Like the sun and moon, we go together. The earth is not capable of existing without both of them, and neither are we. We—"

"Yes." She flung herself into his arms.

Laughing and crying, he crushed her lips with his own.

The light and the dark were meant to be together. And now they would be—here in Dinetah. Forever.

Epilogue

On a sunshine-filled day in late October, two meetings were being held in Dinetah.

The first in honor of two clans. The Big Medicine Clan had come to join with the White Streak People of the Many Cliffs area in celebrating the Blessing Way ceremony.

Hunter had completed placement of a big double-wide mobile home under the cottonwood trees behind Anali's cabin. He was making a home for himself and Bailey on her clan's land, the same way the male members of the Dine had done throughout history.

A few other Navajos had been invited. One—Hunter's former supervisor, Captain Earnest Sam—had just been named the acting director of the Department of Public Safety. He'd been helpful to the Brotherhood when the old Director's death needed to be explained, and they now trusted him completely. Captain Sam was aware of the growing Skinwalker war and would be a good ally for the Brotherhood.

From her wheelchair, Bailey's grandmother sat in silence and watched as the medicine men blessed the house under the tree her grandfather had planted in her name.

Bailey watched her grandmother's face light up with goodwill, while a tear leaked from the corner of her eye. The woman's time had come and gone. It was the Navajo Way.

Then Bailey turned and looked to the man she loved. A new woman's time was now at hand.

Far away, but still on the land between the four sacred mountains, another meeting was taking place.

The Navajo Wolf was furious. For nearly two months he'd been searching for the map. The Dog had betrayed him, hidden the map and then died.

He'd deserved to die for his trickery. But now the precious map was gone.

The Wolf gathered his new lieutenants. "Stop working on everything else," he growled. "Do nothing except search until we locate where the map is hidden. We must have it."

His men did not know, and the Navajo Wolf would not tell them, that the map was the key to their survival.

Without it, they were doomed and would cease to exist. Then there would be a time in Dinetah without the Skinwalkers. A time of peace.

The Wolf would have those scrolls, even if he had to destroy all of Dinetah. Nothing would keep him from his destiny.

* * * * *

*The Brotherhood is keeping watch…and
the Navajo Wolf is on the prowl.
Look for Linda Conrad's next*
NIGHT GUARDIANS *tale, Lucas Tso's story.*
SHADOW SURRENDER
March 2007.
Only from Silhouette Intimate Moments!

Silhouette® Romantic Suspense keeps getting hotter!
Turn the page for a sneak preview of the first book
in Marie Ferrarella's latest miniseries
THE DOCTORS PULASKI

HER LAWMAN ON CALL
by Marie Ferrarella

On sale February 2007 wherever books are sold.

Chapter 1

There was something about a parking structure that always made her feel vulnerable. In broad daylight she found them confusing, and most of the time she had too many other things on her mind. Squeezing in that extra piece of information about where she had left her vehicle sometimes created a mental meltdown.

At night, when there were fewer vehicles housed within this particular parking garage, she felt exposed, helpless. And feelings of déjà vu haunted her. It was a completely irrational reaction and as a physician, she was the first to acknowledge this. But still…

Wanting to run, she moved slowly. She retraced steps she'd taken thirteen hours ago when her day at Patience Memorial Hospital had begun. The lighting down on this level was poor, as one of the bulbs was out, and the air felt heavy and clammy, much like the day had been. Typical

New York City early-autumn weather, she thought. She picked up her pace, making her way toward where she thought she remembered leaving her car, a small, vintage Toyota.

Dr. Sasha Pulaski stripped off her sweater and slung it over her arm, stifling a yawn. The sound of her heels echoed back to her. If she was lucky, she could be sound asleep in less than an hour. Never mind food, she thought. All she wanted was to commune with her pillow and a flat surface—any flat surface—for about six hours.

Not too much to ask, she thought. Unless you were an intern. Mercifully, those days were behind her, but still in front of her two youngest sisters. Five doctors and almost-doctors in one family. Not bad for the offspring of two struggling immigrants who had come into this country with nothing more than the clothes on their backs. She knew that her parents were both proud enough to burst.

A strange, popping noise sounded in the distance. Instantly Sasha stiffened, listening. Holding her breath. Memories suddenly assaulted her.

One hand was clenched at her side, and the other held tightly to the purse strap slung over her shoulder. She willed herself to relax. More than likely, it was just someone from the hospital getting into his car and going home. Or maybe it was one of the security guards, accidentally stepping on something on the ground.

In the past six months, several people had been robbed in and around the structure, and as a result the hospital had beefed up security. There was supposed to be at least one guard making the rounds at all times. That didn't make her feel all that safe. The hairs at the back of her neck stood at attention.

As she rounded the corner, heading toward where she might have left her vehicle, Sasha dug into her purse. Not for her keys, but for the comforting cylindrical shape of the small can of mace her father, Josef Pulaski, a retired NYPD police officer, insisted that she and her sisters carry with them at all times. Her fingers tightened around the small dispenser just as she saw a short, squat man up ahead. He had a mop of white hair, a kindly face and, even in his uniform, looked as if he could be a stand-in for a mall Santa Claus.

The security guard, she thought in relief, her fingers growing lax. She'd seen him around and even exchanged a few words with him on occasion. He was retired, with no family. Being a guard gave him something to do, a reason to get up each day.

The next moment, her relief began to slip away. The guard was looking down at something on the ground. There was a deep frown on his face and his body was rigid, as if frozen in place.

Sasha picked up her pace. "Mr. Stevens?" she called out. "Is something wrong?"

His head jerked in her direction. He seemed startled to see her. Or was that horror on his face?

Before she could ask him any more questions, Sasha saw what had robbed him of his speech. There was the body of a woman lying beside a car. Blood pooled beneath her head, streaming toward her frayed tan trench coat. A look of surprise was forever frozen on her pretty, bronze features.

Recognition was immediate. A scream, wide and thick, lodged itself in Sasha's throat as she struggled not to release it.

Angela. One of her colleagues.

She'd talked to Angela a little more than two hours ago. Terror vibrated through Sasha's very being.

How?

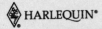

This February...

Catch NASCAR Superstar **Carl Edwards** in

SPEED DATING!

Kendall assesses risk for a living—so she's the last person you'd expect to see on the arm of a race-car driver who thrives on the unpredictable. But when a bizarre turn of events—and NASCAR hotshot Dylan Hargreave—inspire her to trade in her ever-so-structured existence for "life in the fast lane" she starts to feel she might be on to something!

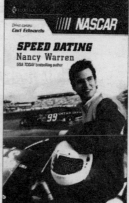

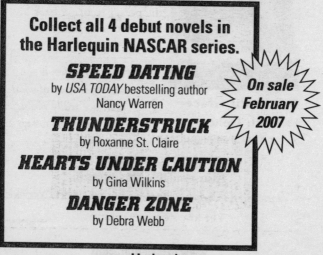

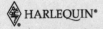

HARLEQUIN®

E V E R L A S T I N G L O V E™

Every great love has a story to tell™

Save $1.⁰⁰ off

the purchase of
any Harlequin
Everlasting Love novel

Coupon valid from January 1, 2007
until April 30, 2007.

Valid at retail outlets in the U.S. only.
Limit one coupon per customer.

5 65373 00076 2   (8100) 0 11302

HEUSCPN0407

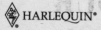

EVERLASTING LOVE™

Every great love has a story to tell™

Save $1.⁰⁰ off

the purchase of any Harlequin Everlasting Love novel

Coupon valid from January 1, 2007 until April 30, 2007.

Valid at retail outlets in Canada only. Limit one coupon per customer.

52607370

HECDNCPN0407

REQUEST YOUR FREE BOOKS!

2 FREE NOVELS PLUS 2 FREE GIFTS!

Silhouette® Romantic

SUSPENSE

Sparked by Danger, Fueled by Passion!

YES! Please send me 2 FREE Silhouette® Romantic Suspense novels and my 2 FREE gifts. After receiving them, if I don't wish to receive any more books, I can return the shipping statement marked "cancel." If I don't cancel, I will receive 4 brand-new novels every month and be billed just $4.24 per book in the U.S., or $4.99 per book in Canada, plus 25¢ shipping and handling per book plus applicable taxes, if any*. That's a savings of at least 15% off the cover price! I understand that accepting the 2 free books and gifts places me under no obligation to buy anything. I can always return a shipment and cancel at any time. Even if I never buy another book from Silhouette, the two free books and gifts are mine to keep forever.

240 SDN EEX6 340 SDN EEYJ

Name _____ (PLEASE PRINT)

Address _____ Apt. #

City _____ State/Prov. _____ Zip/Postal Code

Signature (if under 18, a parent or guardian must sign)

Mail to the **Silhouette Reader Service™:**
IN U.S.A.: P.O. Box 1867, Buffalo, NY 14240-1867
IN CANADA: P.O. Box 609, Fort Erie, Ontario L2A 5X3

Not valid to current Silhouette Intimate Moments subscribers.

Want to try two free books from another line?
Call 1-800-873-8635 or visit www.morefreebooks.com.

* Terms and prices subject to change without notice. NY residents add applicable sales tax. Canadian residents will be charged applicable provincial taxes and GST. This offer is limited to one order per household. All orders subject to approval. Credit or debit balances in a customer's account(s) may be offset by any other outstanding balance owed by or to the customer. Please allow 4 to 6 weeks for delivery.

Your Privacy: Silhouette is committed to protecting your privacy. Our Privacy Policy is available online at www.eHarlequin.com or upon request from the Reader Service. From time to time we make our lists of customers available to reputable firms who may have a product or service of interest to you. If you would prefer we not share your name and address, please check here. ☐

SRS07

Silhouette®

COMING NEXT MONTH

#1451 HER LAWMAN ON CALL—Marie Ferrarella
The Doctors Pulaski
Discovering a dead colleague is no way to end a grueling day at the hospital, but Dr. Sasha Pulaski has other problems when the detective on the case plays guardian angel—and tempts her desires.

#1452 DARK REUNION—Justine Davis
Redstone, Incorporated
Security agent Reeve Fox just faced a ghost—Zach Westin, father of the murdered boy she hadn't been fast enough to save. Now they must work together to save a missing teen—and deal with an attraction that's still blazing.

#1453 MORE THAN A HERO—Marilyn Pappano
True-crime novelist Jake Norris wants to write about a long-standing murder. But when his main suspect—now a distinguished senator—won't cooperate, Jake turns to the man's captivating daughter for help. Could her family secret destroy their future?

#1454 THE FORBIDDEN ENCHANTMENT—Nina Bruhns
After being dead for two hundred years, an infamous pirate wakes up in the twenty-first-century body of fire chief Andre Sullivan. With a serial arsonist on the loose, Sully must uncover the culprit, while curtailing his attraction to the one woman who can reveal the truth about his past.